ST...P!

...S TWO STORIES — ONE BLUE AND ONE RED — BUT YOU CAN READ IT MANY DIFFERENT WAYS . . .

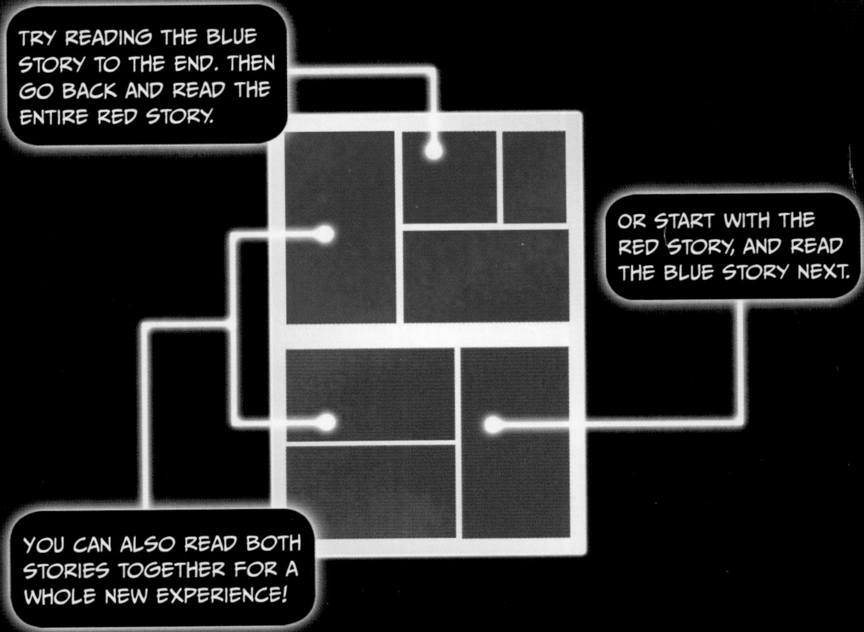
TRY READING THE BLUE STORY TO THE END. THEN GO BACK AND READ THE ENTIRE RED STORY.
OR START WITH THE RED STORY, AND READ THE BLUE STORY NEXT.
YOU CAN ALSO READ BOTH STORIES TOGETHER FOR A WHOLE NEW EXPERIENCE!

IT'S UP TO YOU!

READ THIS BOOK AGAIN AND AGAIN TO DISCOVER EXCITING, NEW DETAILS IN THE NEVER-ENDING BATTLE OF . . . GOOD VS EVIL.

ALIEN
SNOW

by
Michael Dahl

illustrated by
Roberta Pares

STONE ARCH BOOKS
a capstone imprint

Story by Michael Dahl
Illustrated by Roberta Pares
Color by Glass House Graphics
Series Designer: Brann Garvey
Series Editor: Donald Lemke
Editorial Director: Michael Dahl
Art Director: Bob Lentz
Creative Director: Heather Kindseth

WWW.CAPSTONEPUB.COM

Good vs Evil is published by Stone Arch Books,
1710 Roe Crest Drive, North Mankato, Minnesota 56003

Library of Congress Cataloging-in-Publication Data
Dahl, Michael.
Alien snow / written by Michael Dahl ; illustrated by Glass House Graphics.
p. cm. -- (Good vs. evil)
ISBN 978-1-4342-2090-5 (library binding)
ISBN 978-1-4342-3444-5 (paperback)
1. Graphic novels. [1. Graphic novels. 2. Extraterrestrial beings--Fiction. 3. Good and evil--Fiction. 4. Stories without words.] I. Glass House Graphics. II. Title.
PZ7.7.D34Al 2011
741.5'973--dc22
2010004111

Summary: On a winter day, a young boy visits a strange antique shop. The eerie shopkeeper tries to interest the boy in his personal collection of snow globes. The boy is polite, but clearly bored by the objects. Then suddenly, the boy finds himself trapped inside one of the globes — another prisoner in the shopkeeper's collection. The boy must find a way to escape, or remain trapped forever!

PRINTED IN THE UNITED STATES OF AMERICA IN NORTH MANKATO, MINNESOTA.
012017 010252R

"I DON'T BELIEVE THAT THERE ARE
ALIENS. I JUST BELIEVE THERE ARE
REALLY DIFFERENT PEOPLE."

—ORSON SCOTT CARD

THE SHOPKEEPER

NO ONE NOTICED THAT A NEW SHOP OPENED IN A QUIET PART OF THE CITY – "ONE OF A KIND." NO ONE SAW ITS MYSTERIOUS SHOPKEEPER BEFORE TODAY, EITHER. PERHAPS THE SHOPKEEPER DOESN'T LIKE CROWDS. HE MIGHT BE LOOKING FOR JUST A FEW SPECIAL CUSTOMERS . . .

GOOD vs EVIL

NOAH URBAIN

EVERYONE SAYS THAT YOUNG NOAH IS ONE OF A KIND. HIS HEAD IS IN THE CLOUDS. HE IS TEASED BECAUSE HE LIKES TO DREAM ABOUT ALIENS AND OUTER SPACE. BUT HIS SPECIAL INTERESTS IN ASTRONAUTS AND SCIENCE MIGHT JUST SAVE HIS LIFE . . .

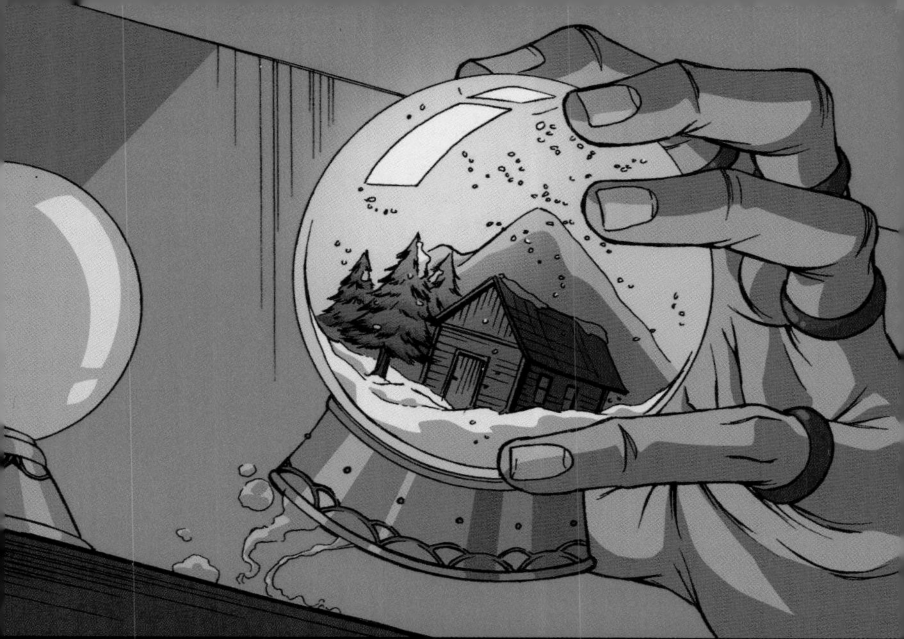

7

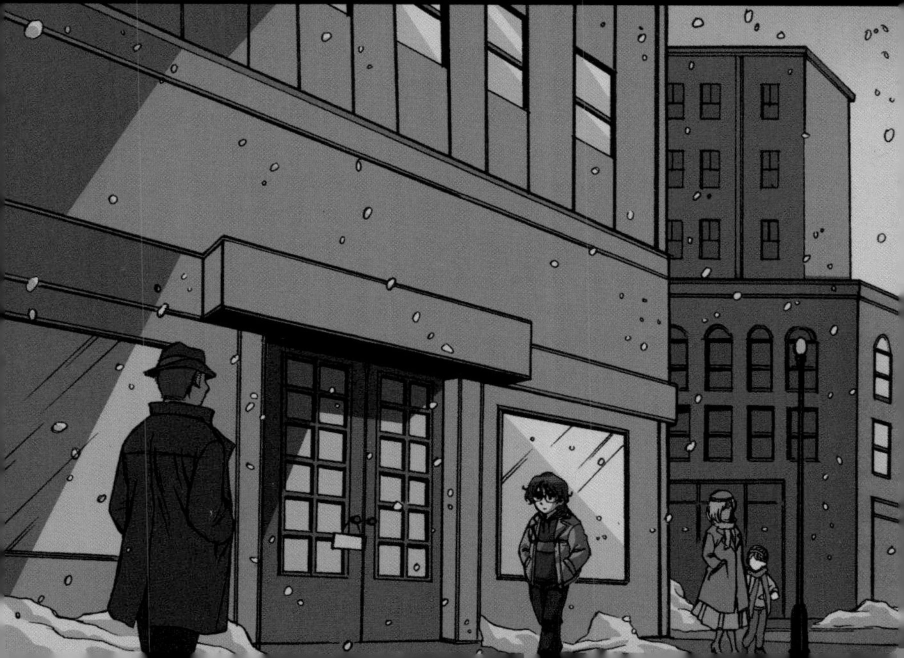

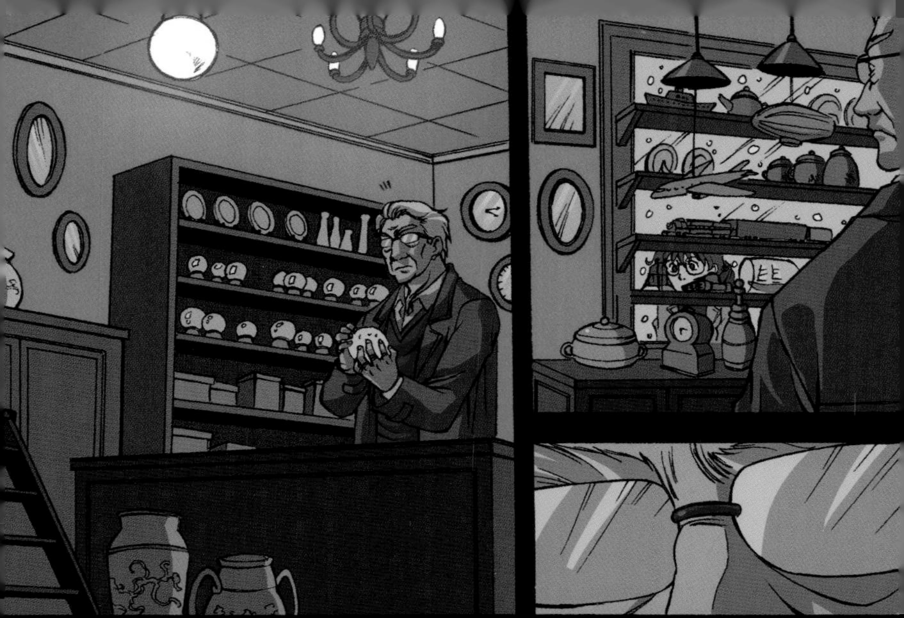

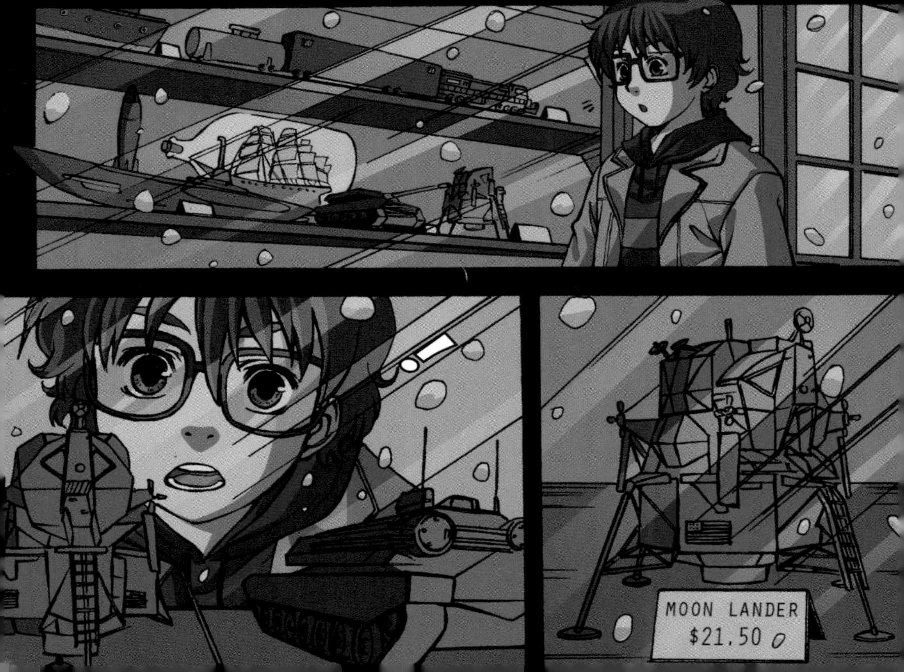

MOON LANDER
$21.50

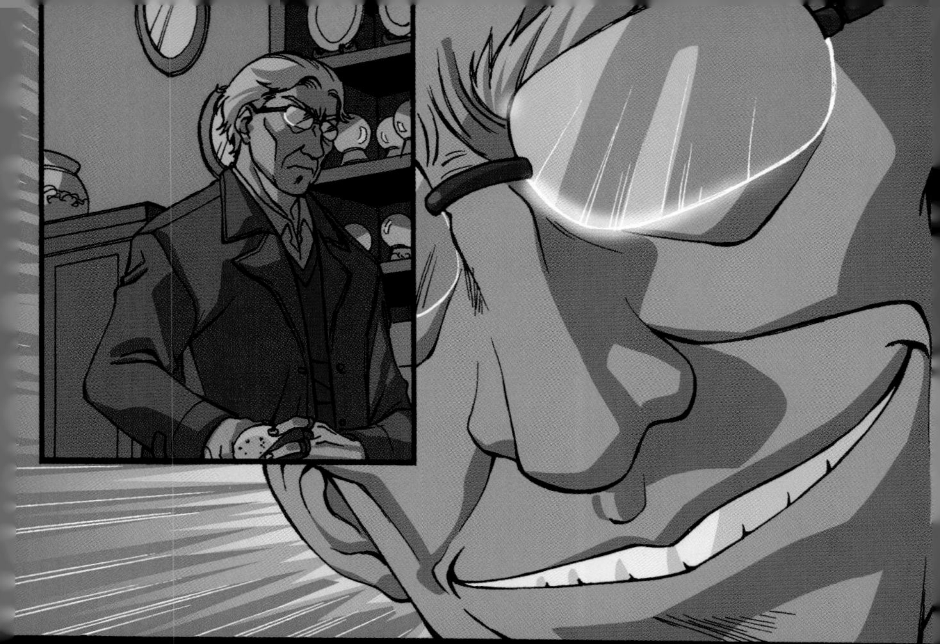

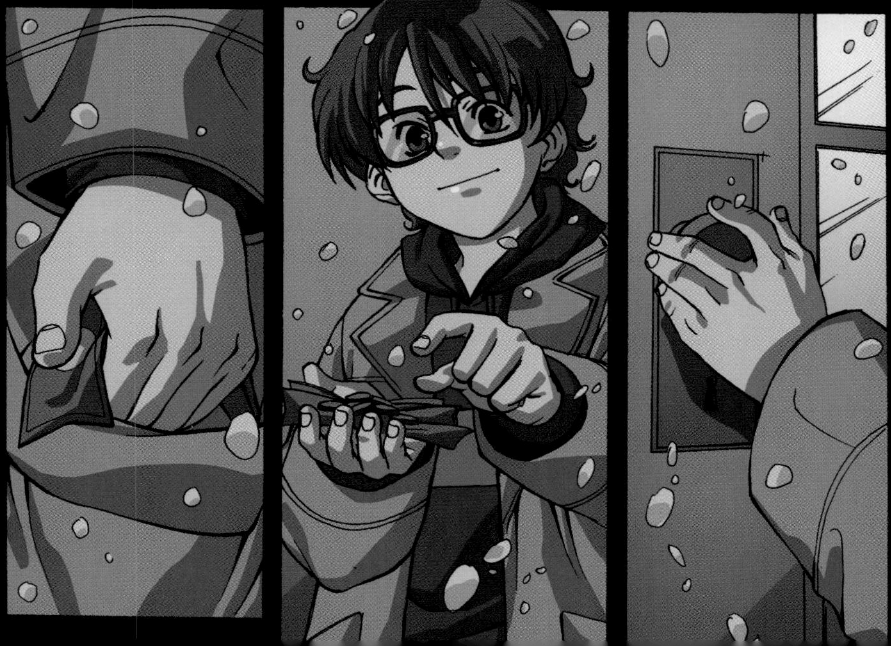

WELCOME. ARE YOU HERE FOR THE GLOBE?

NO, I—

—I WANT TO BUY THE MOON LANDER.

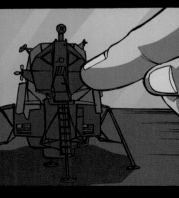

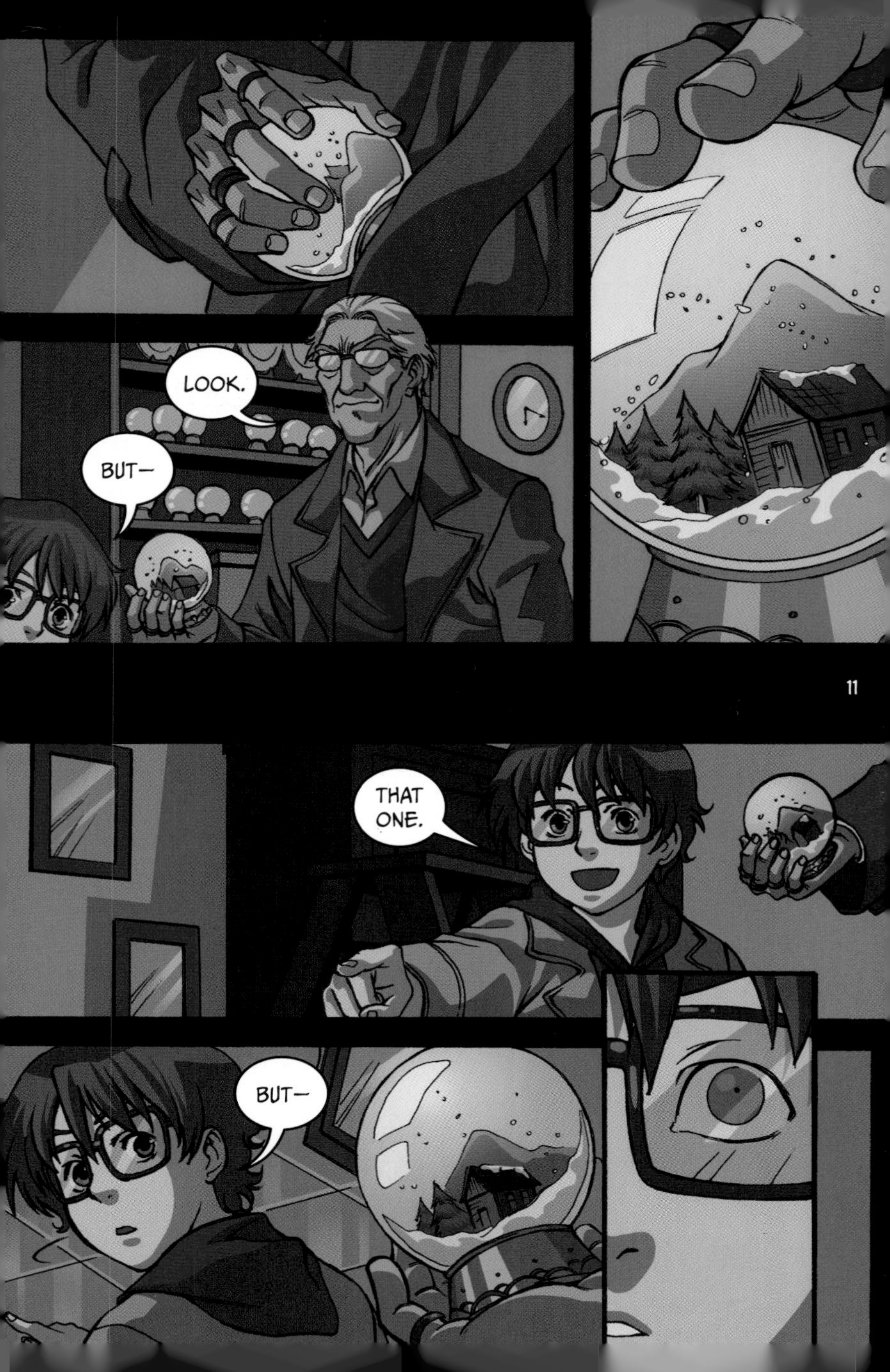
LOOK.
BUT—
THAT ONE.
BUT—

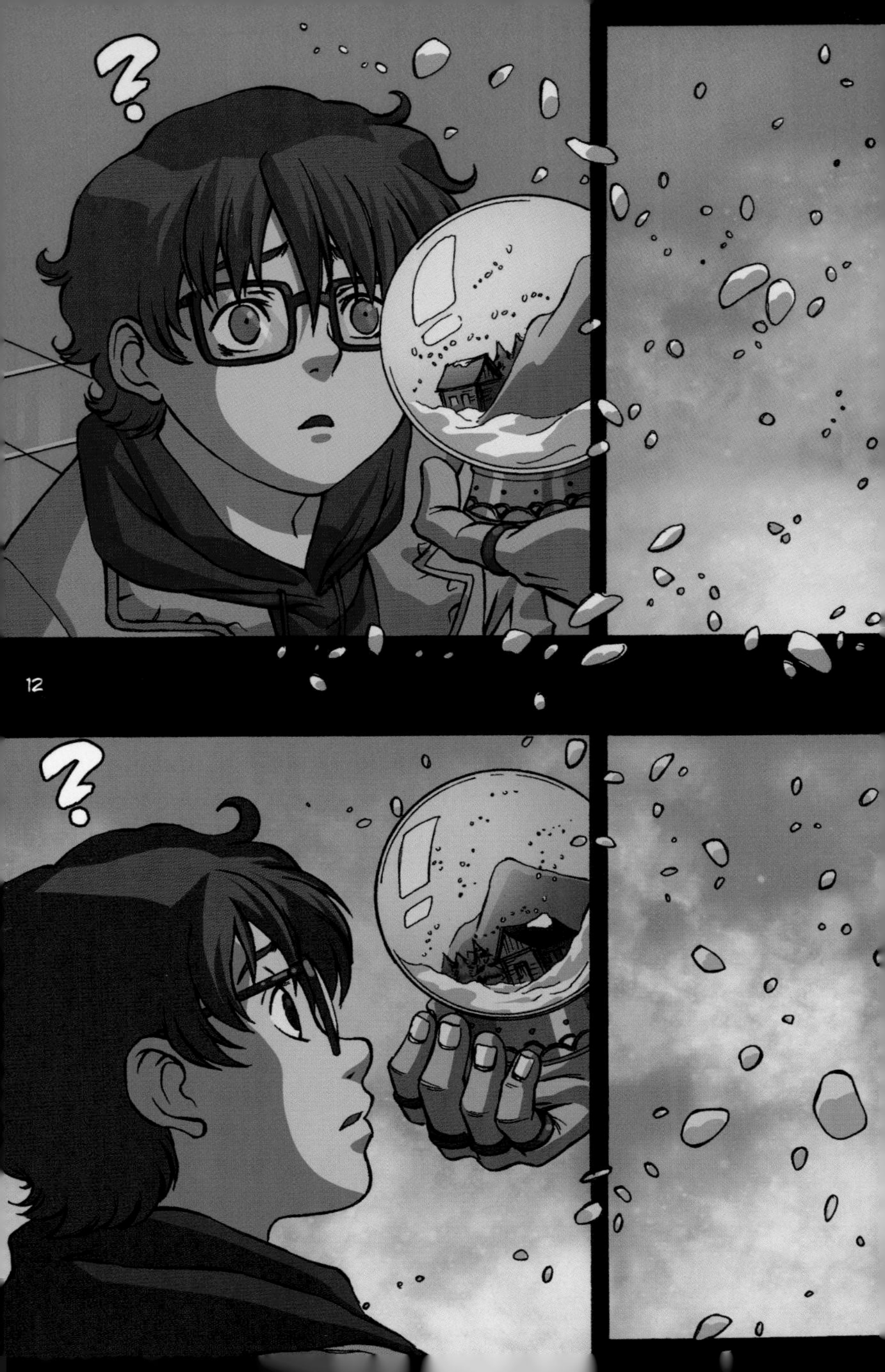
?
?

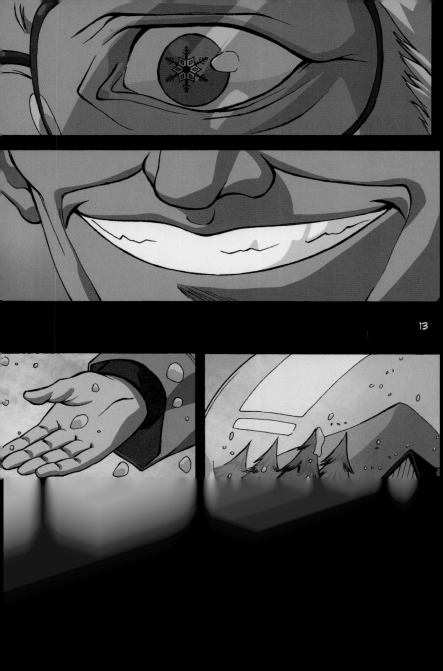

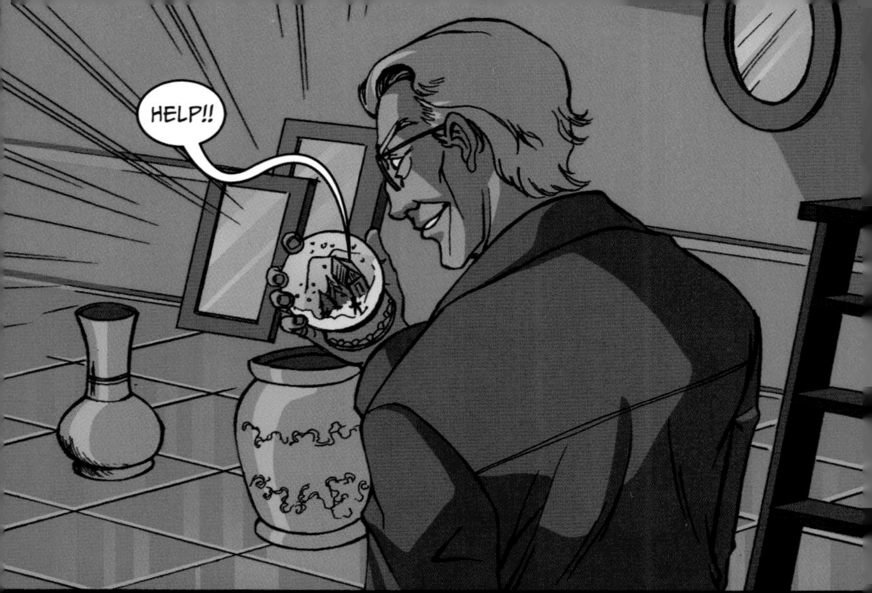
HELP!!

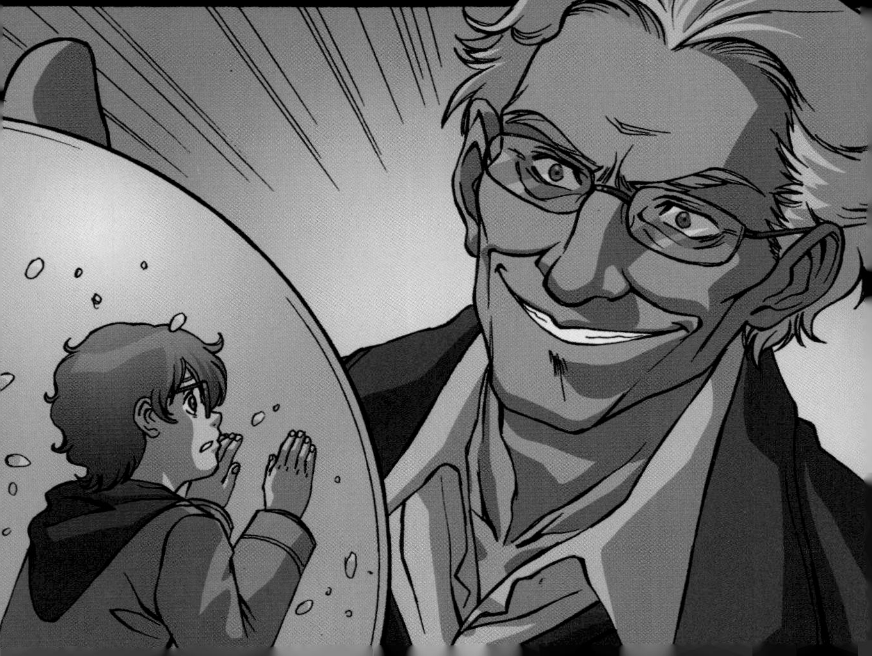

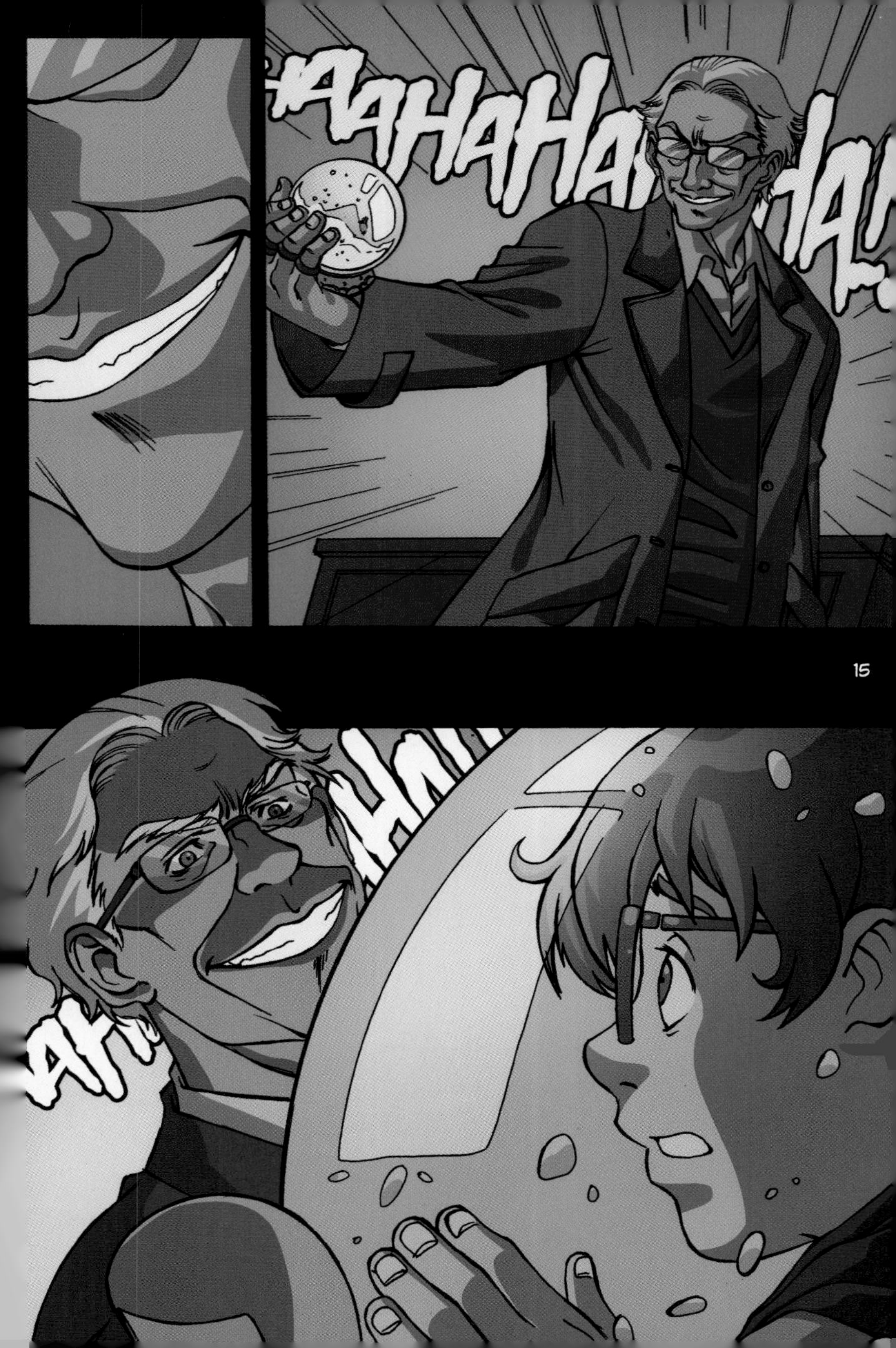

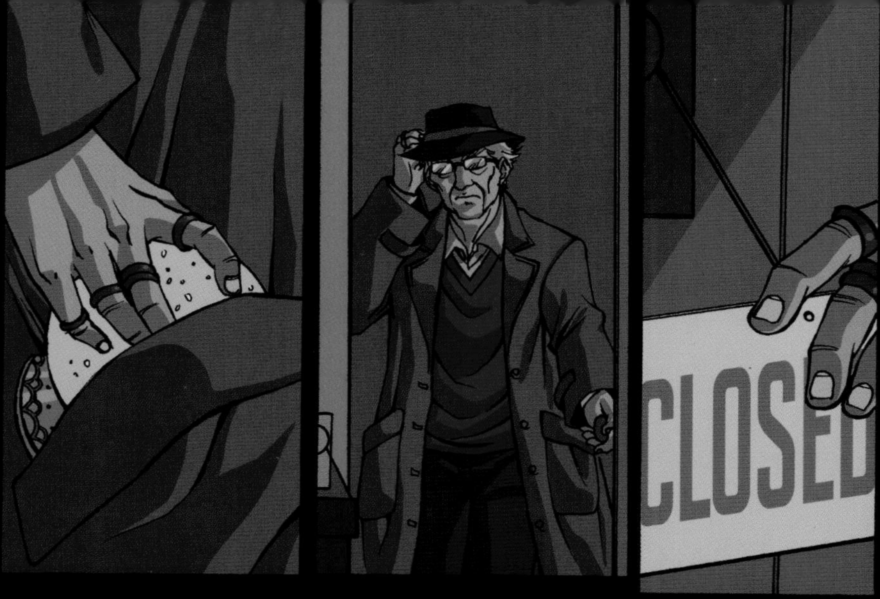
CLOSED

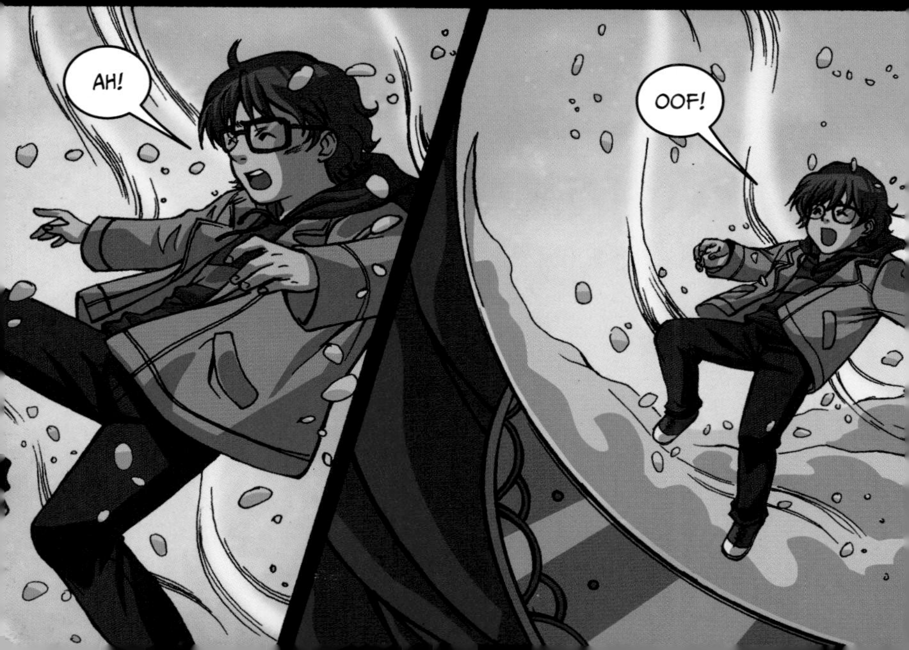
AH!
OOF!

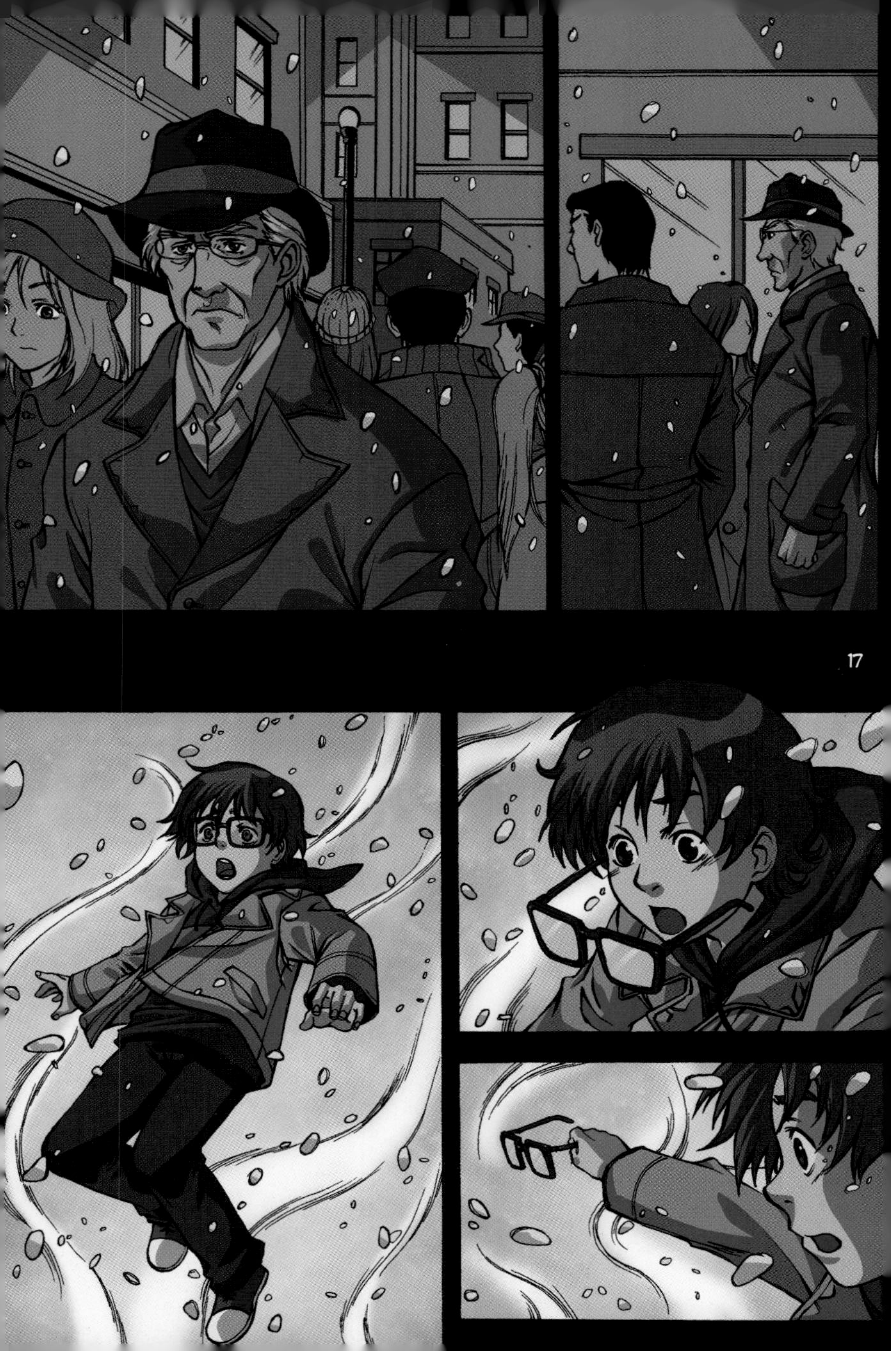

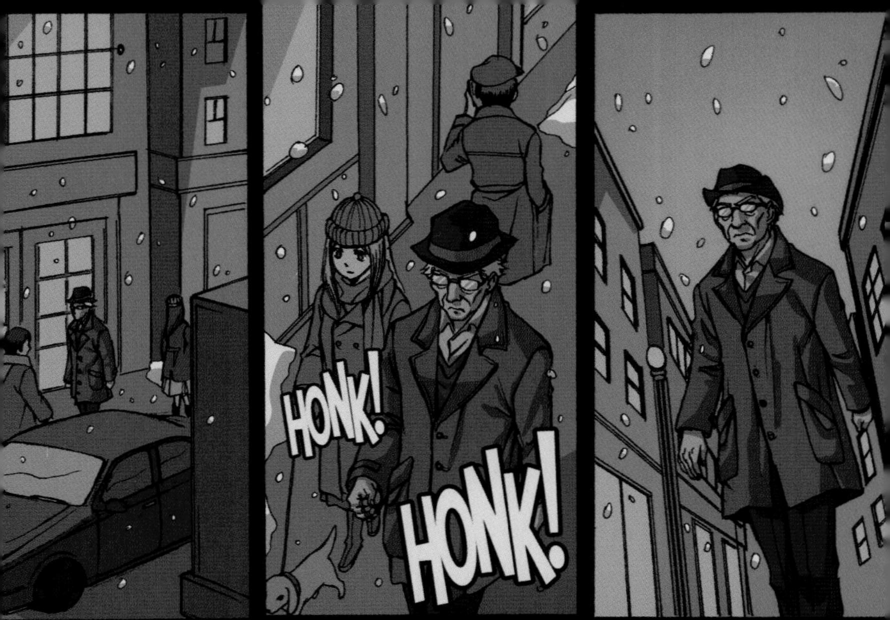
HONK!
HONK!

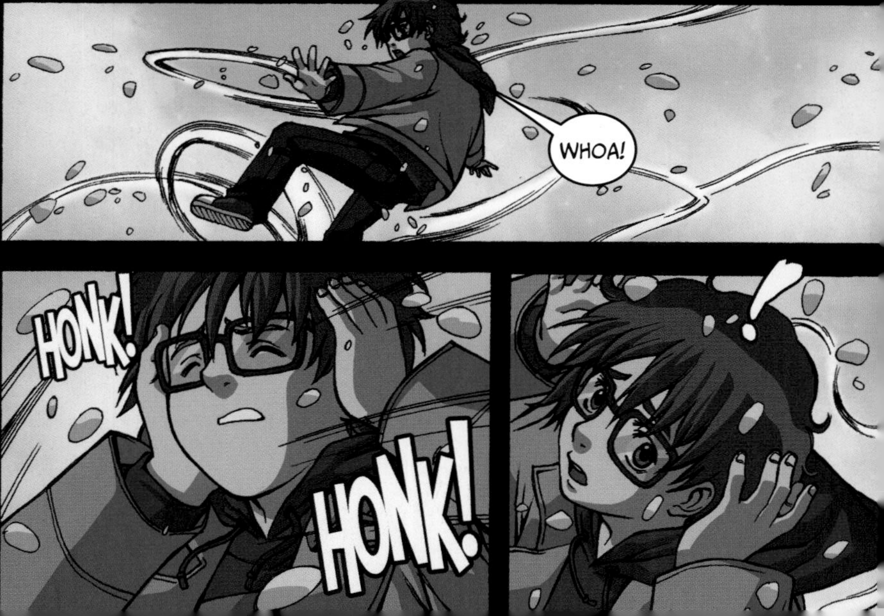
WHOA!
HONK!
HONK!
!

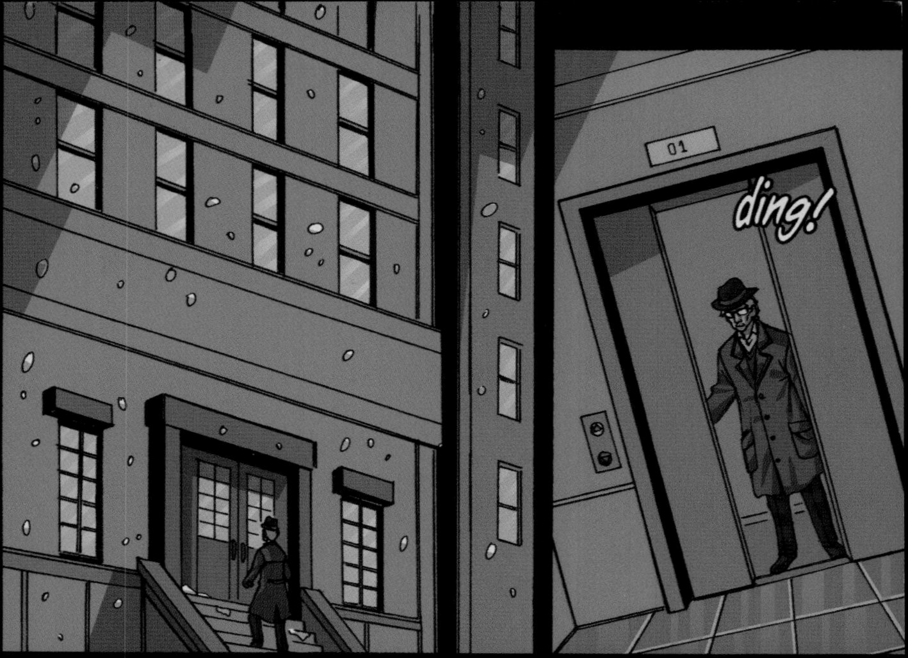
01
ding!

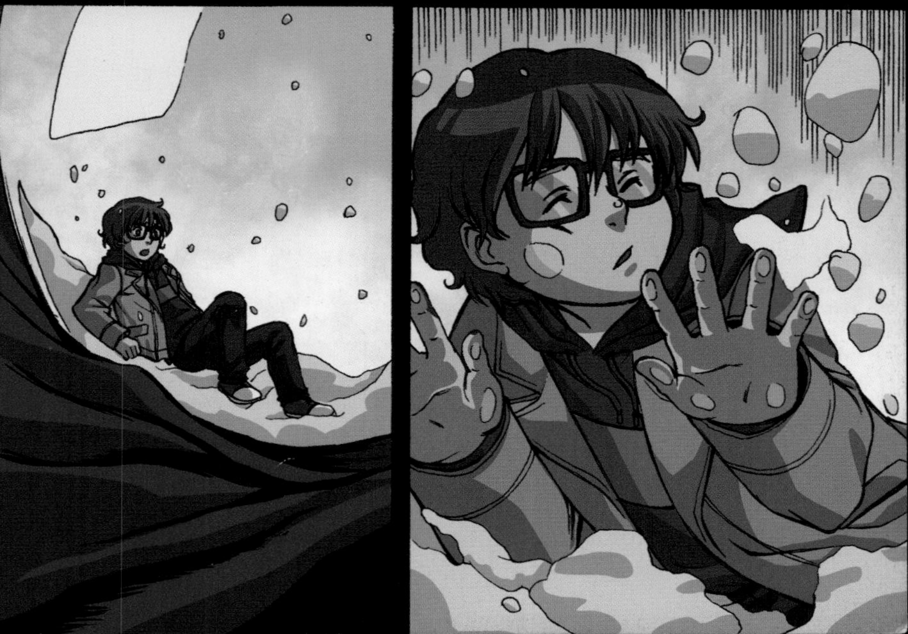

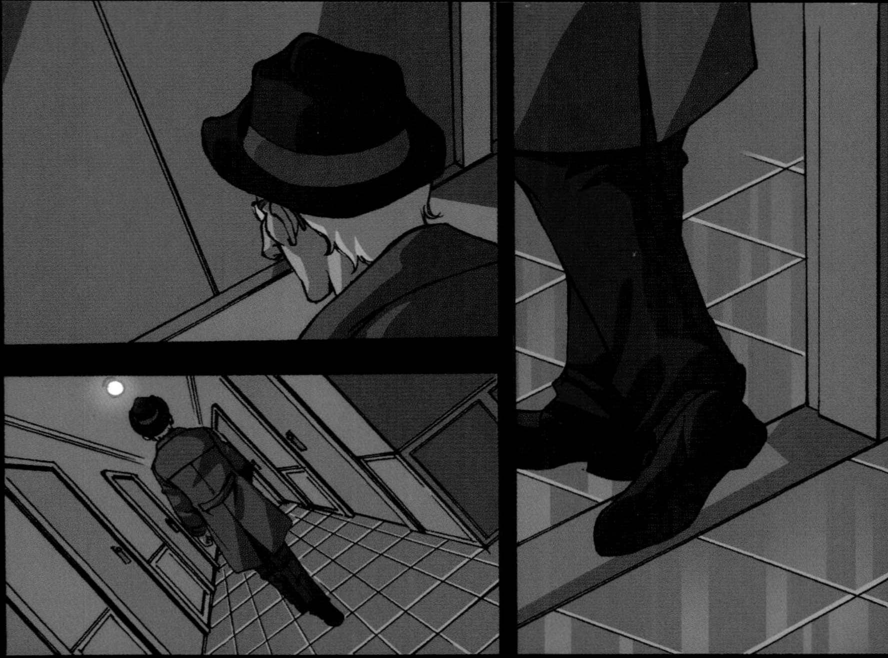

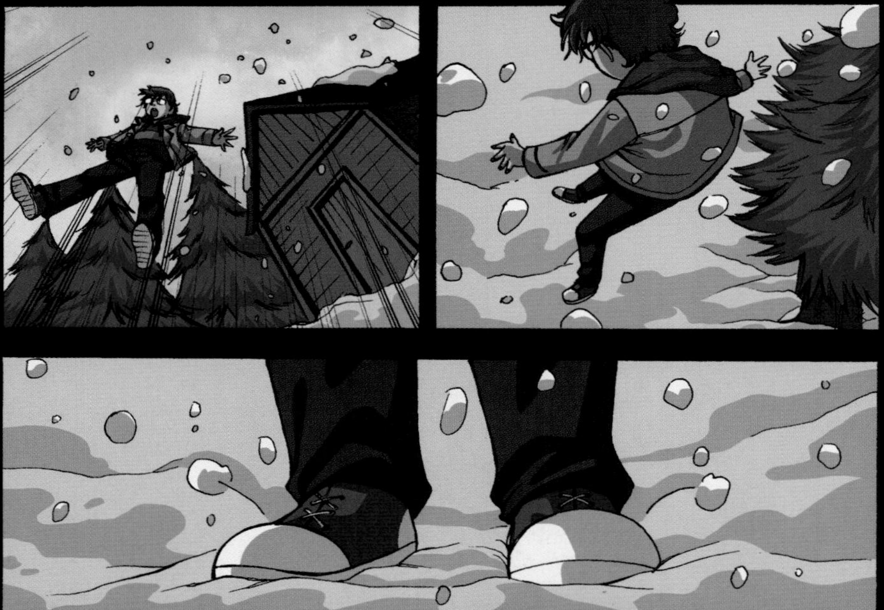

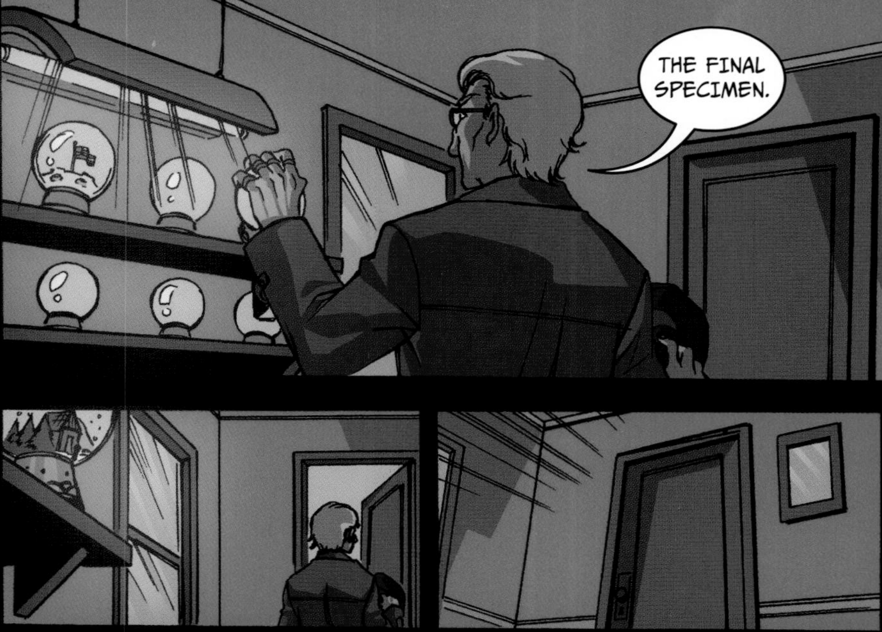
THE FINAL SPECIMEN.

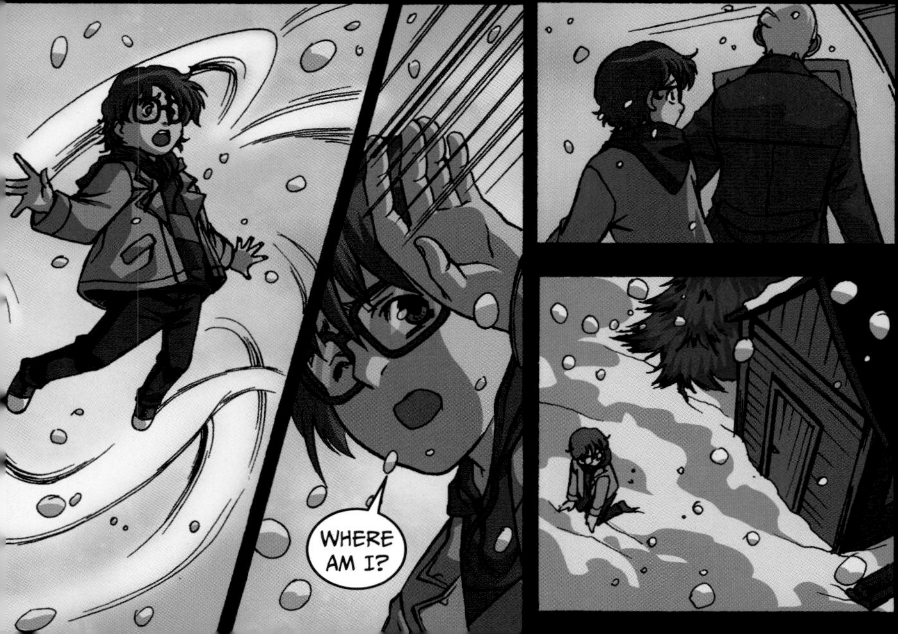
WHERE AM I?

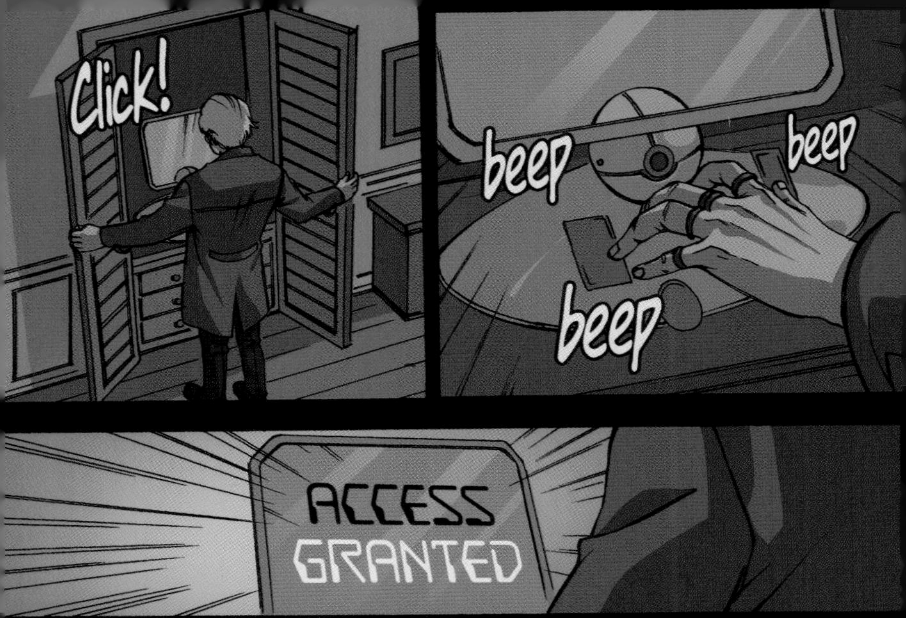
Click!
beep
beep
beep
ACCESS
GRANTED

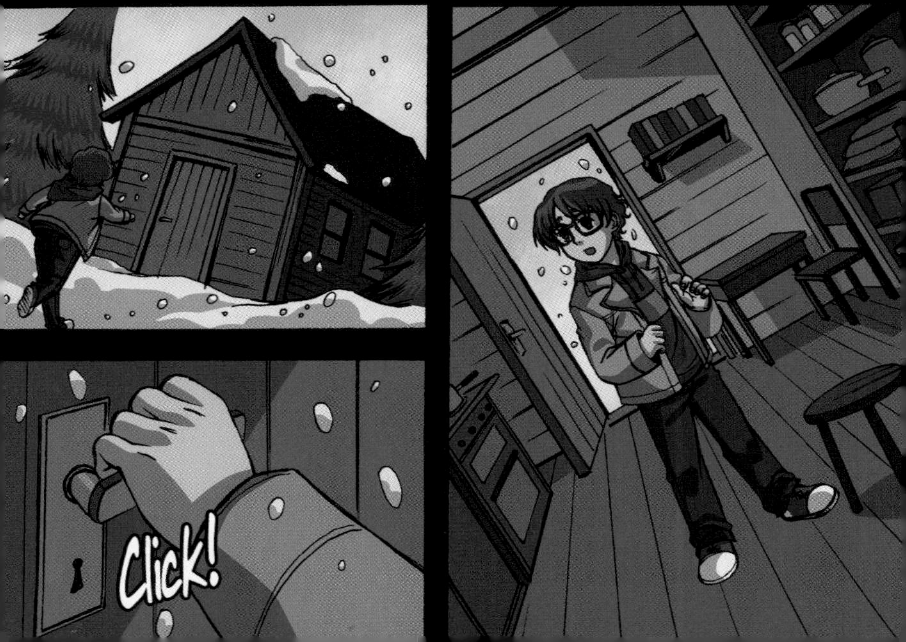
Click!

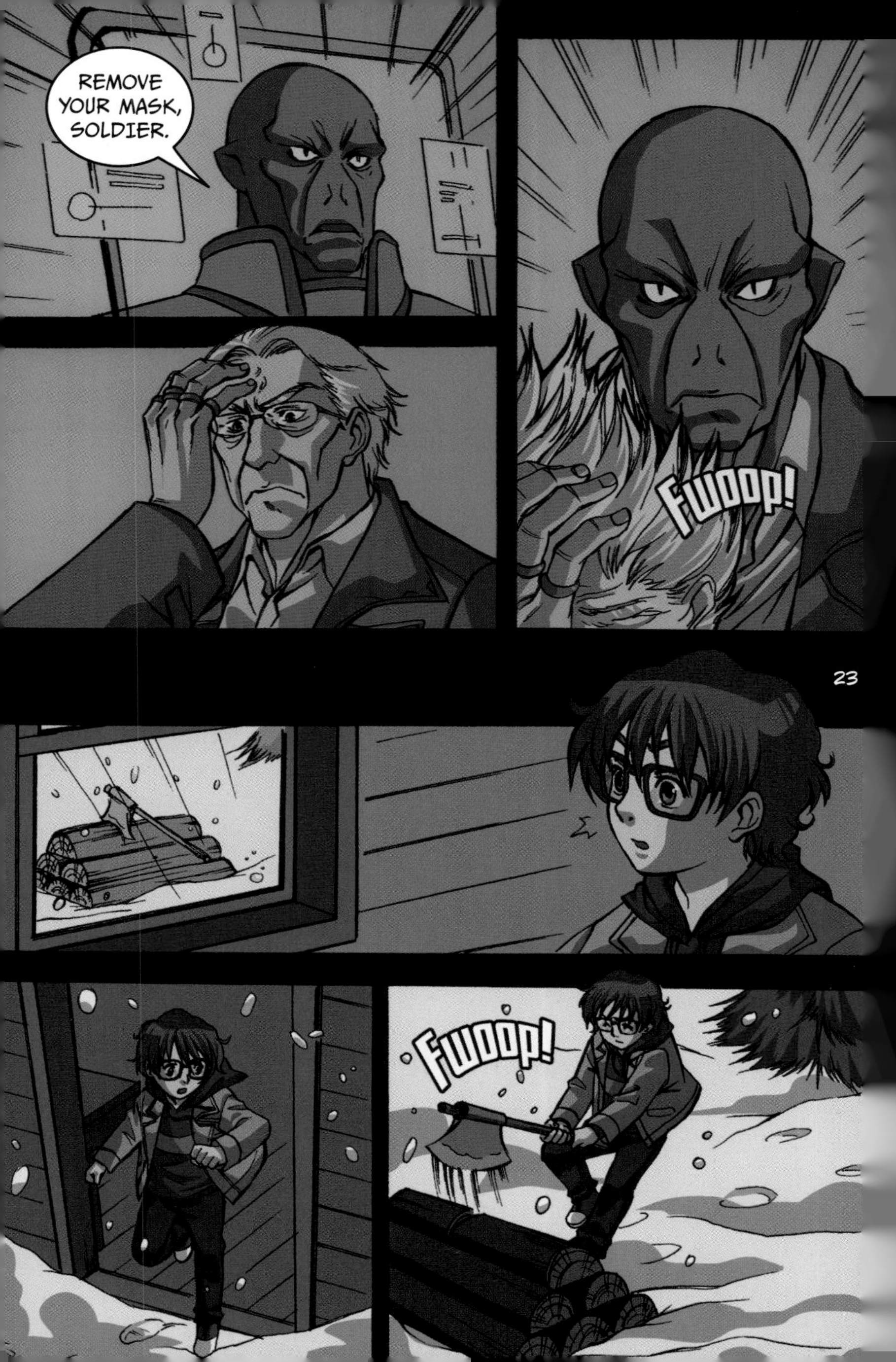
REMOVE YOUR MASK, SOLDIER.
FWOOP!
FWOOP!

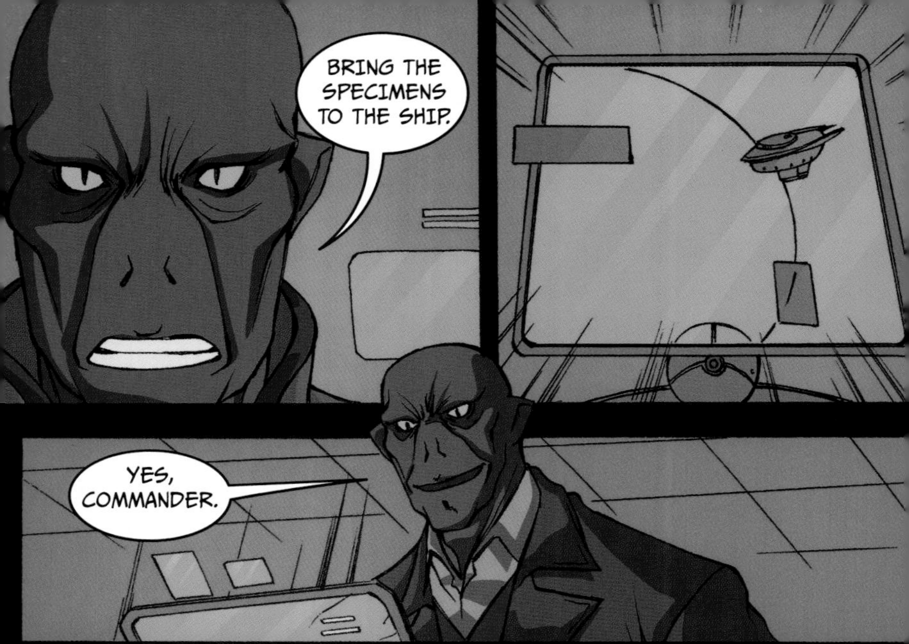
BRING THE SPECIMENS TO THE SHIP.
YES, COMMANDER.

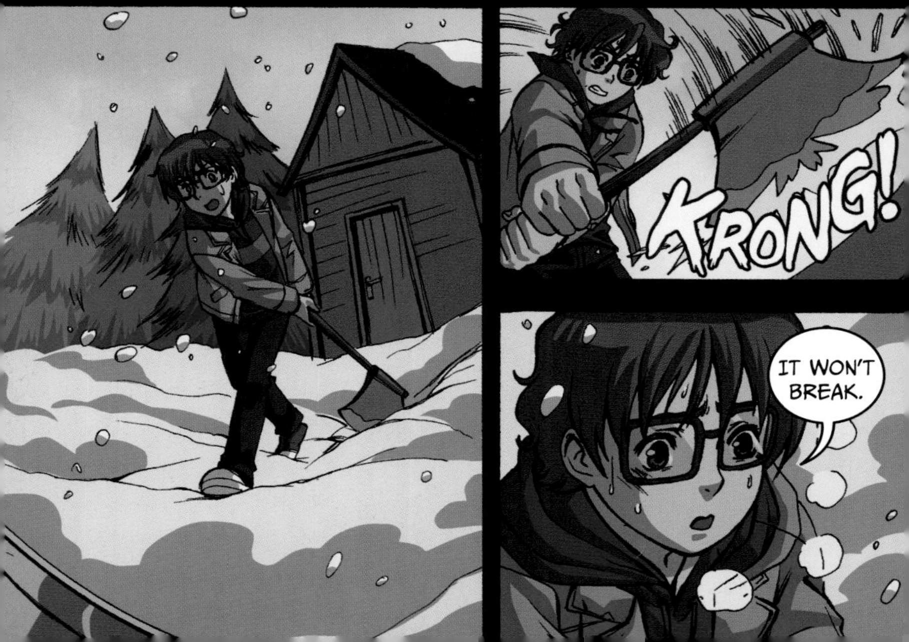
KRONG!
IT WON'T BREAK.

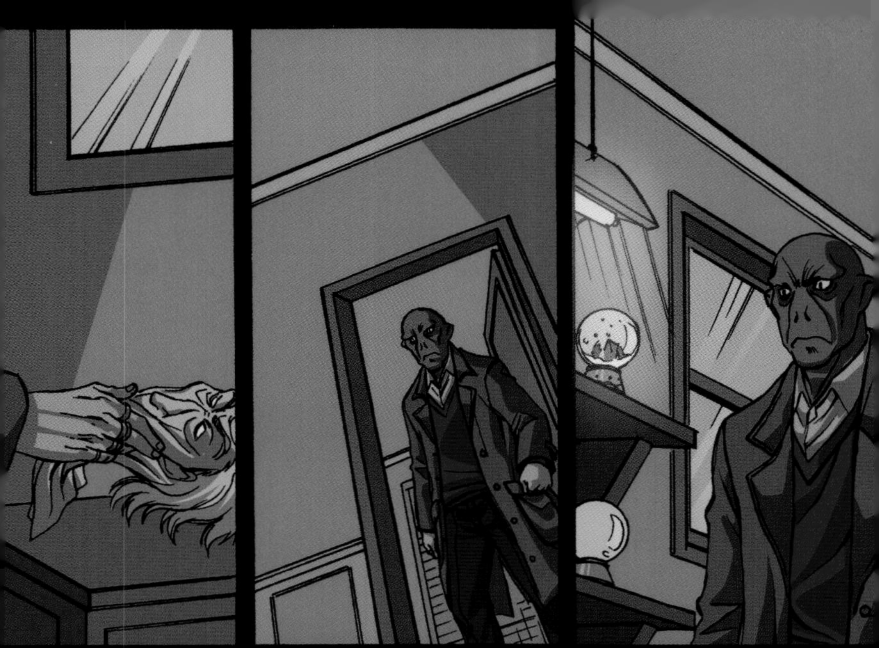

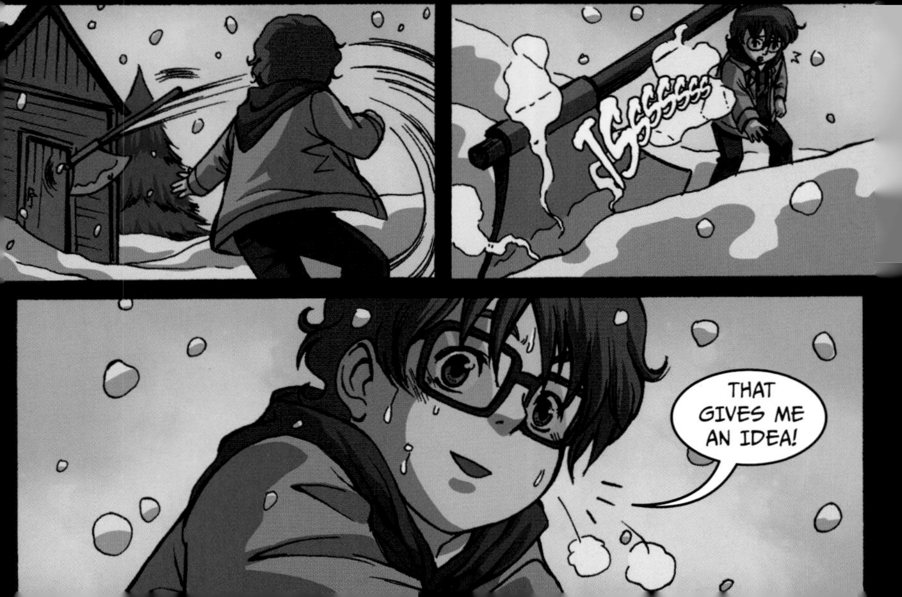
TSSSSSS
THAT GIVES ME AN IDEA!

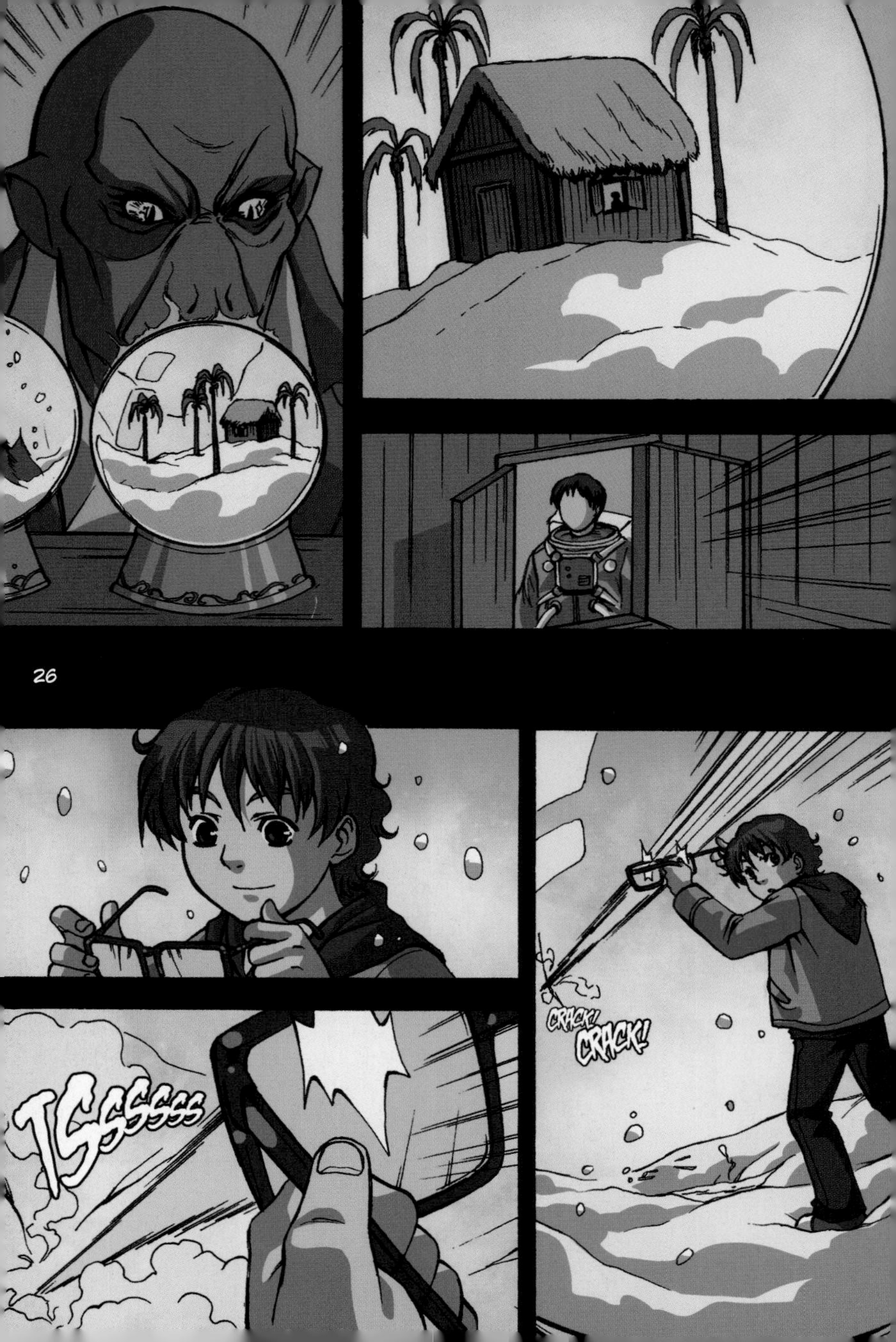
TSSSSSS
CRACK!
CRACK!

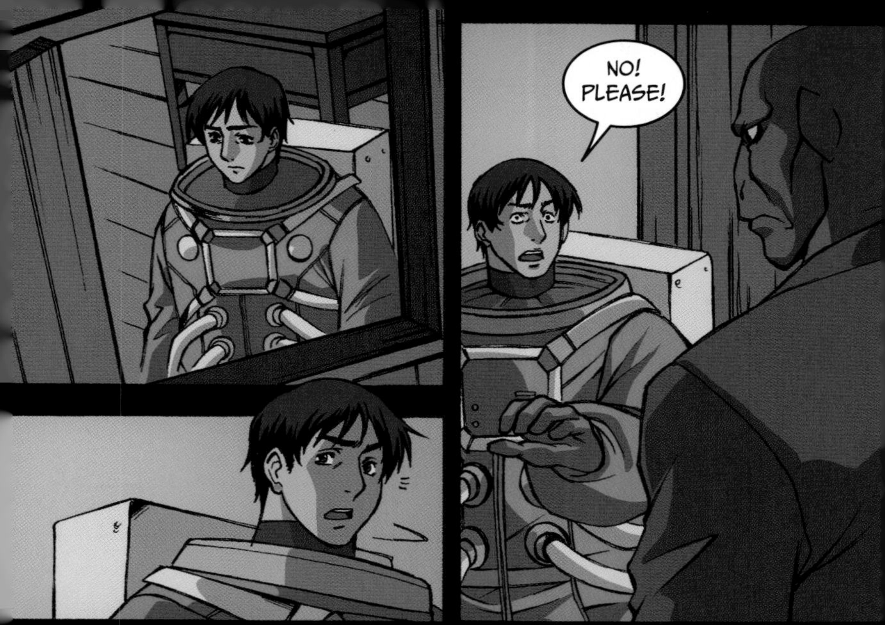
NO!
PLEASE!

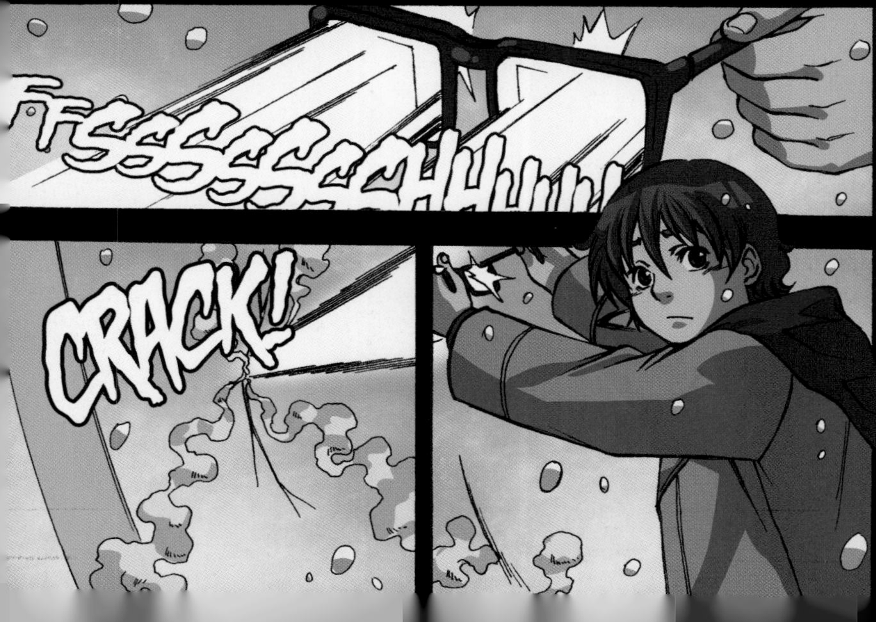
FFSSSSSCHHHHHH
CRACK!

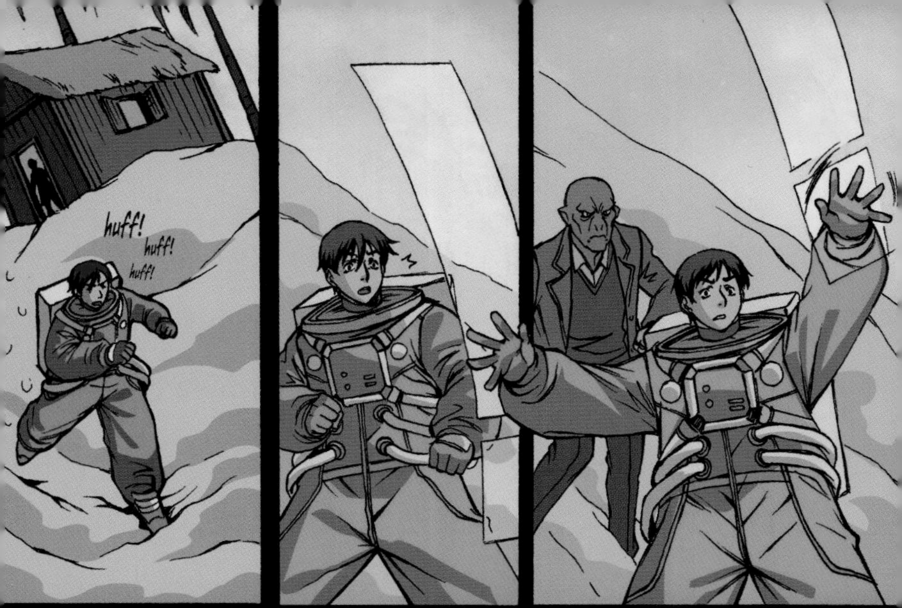
huff!
huff!
huff!

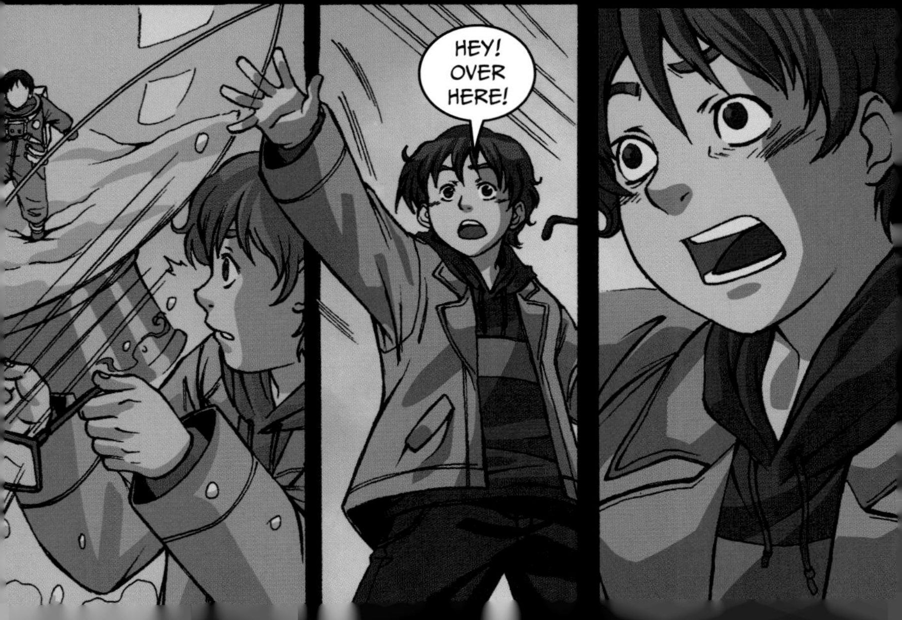
HEY! OVER HERE!

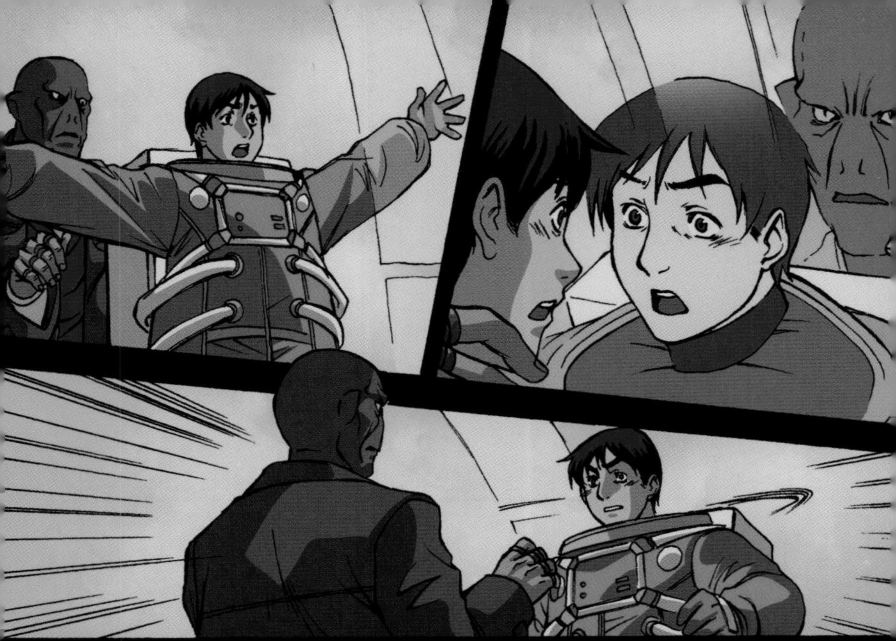

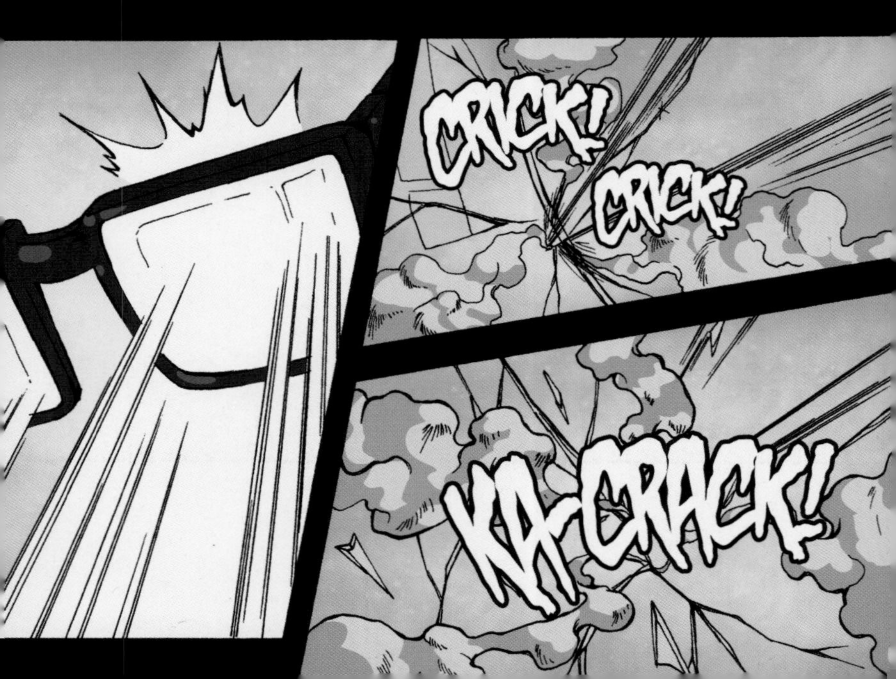
CRICK!
CRICK!
KA-CRACK!

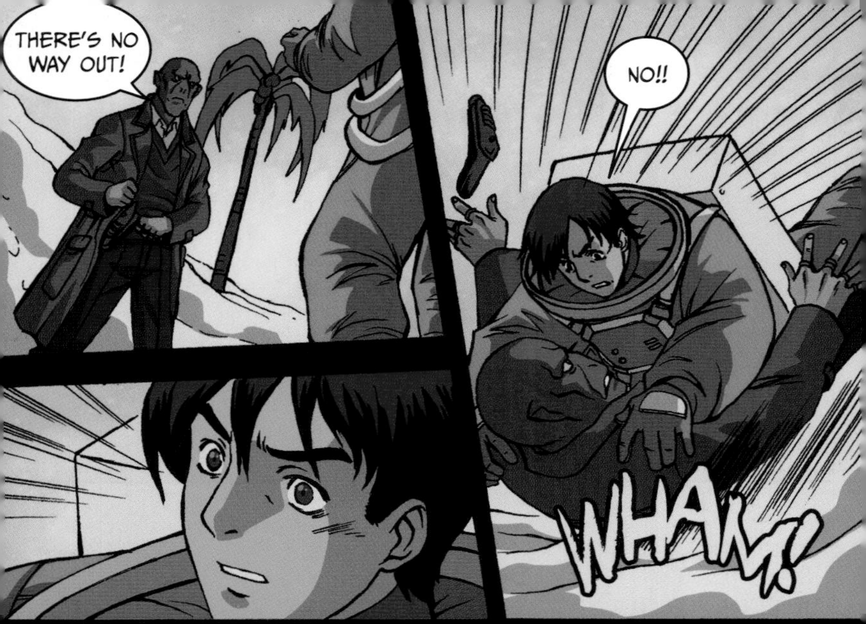
THERE'S NO WAY OUT!
NO!!
WHAM!

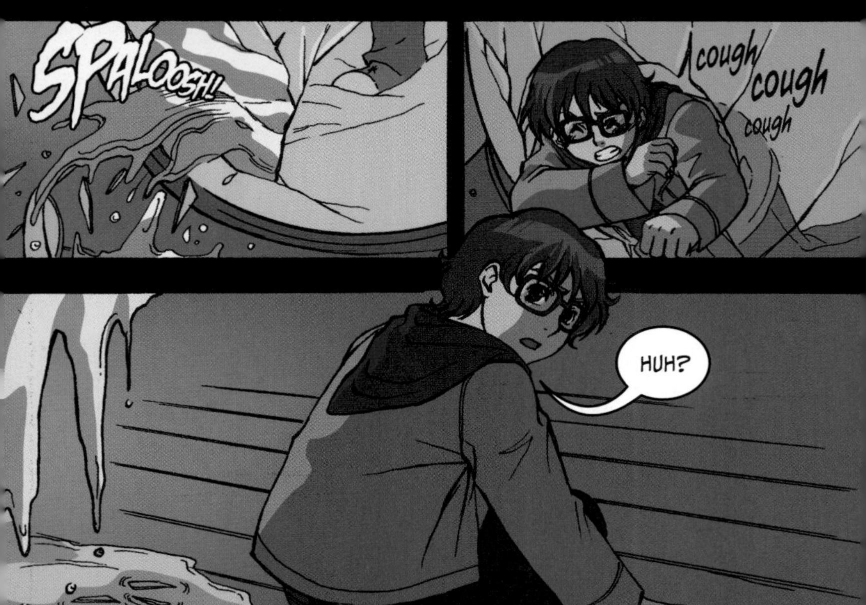
SPALOOSH!
cough
cough
cough
HUH?

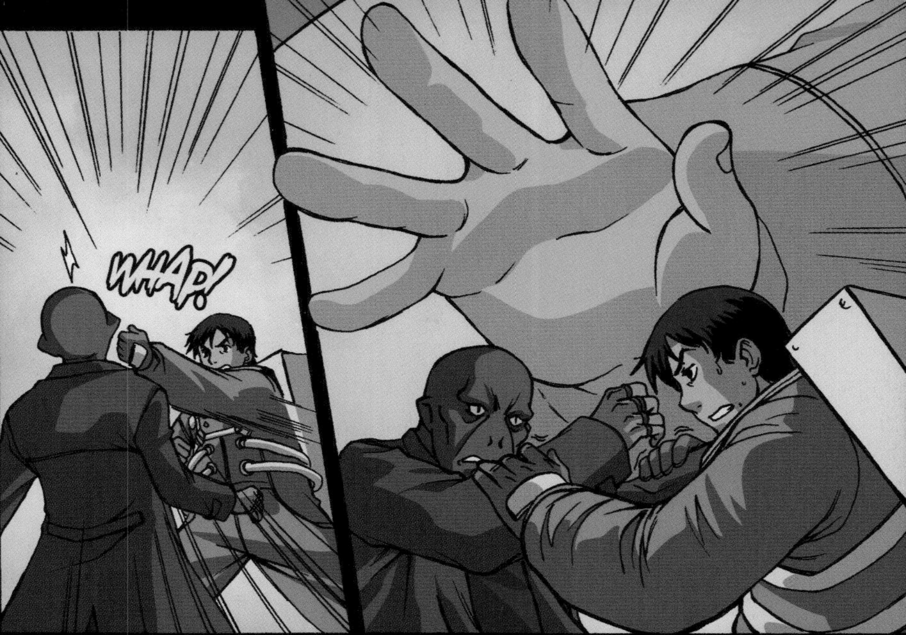
WHAP!

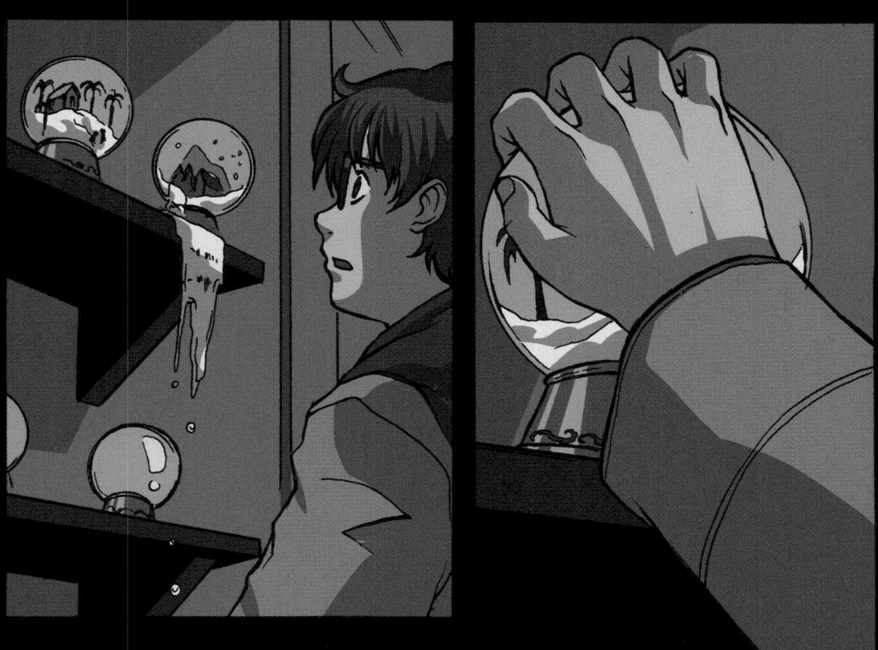

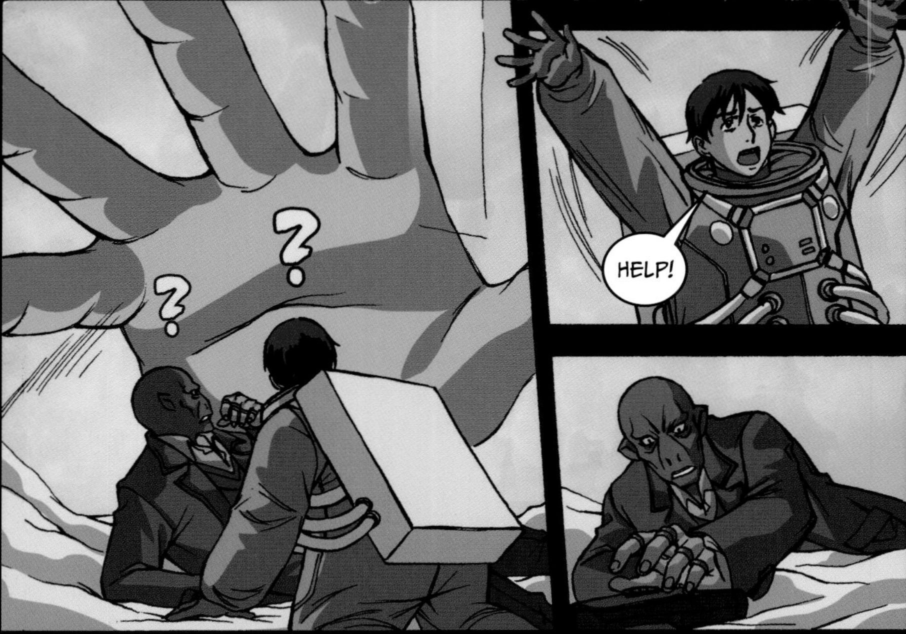
?
?
HELP!

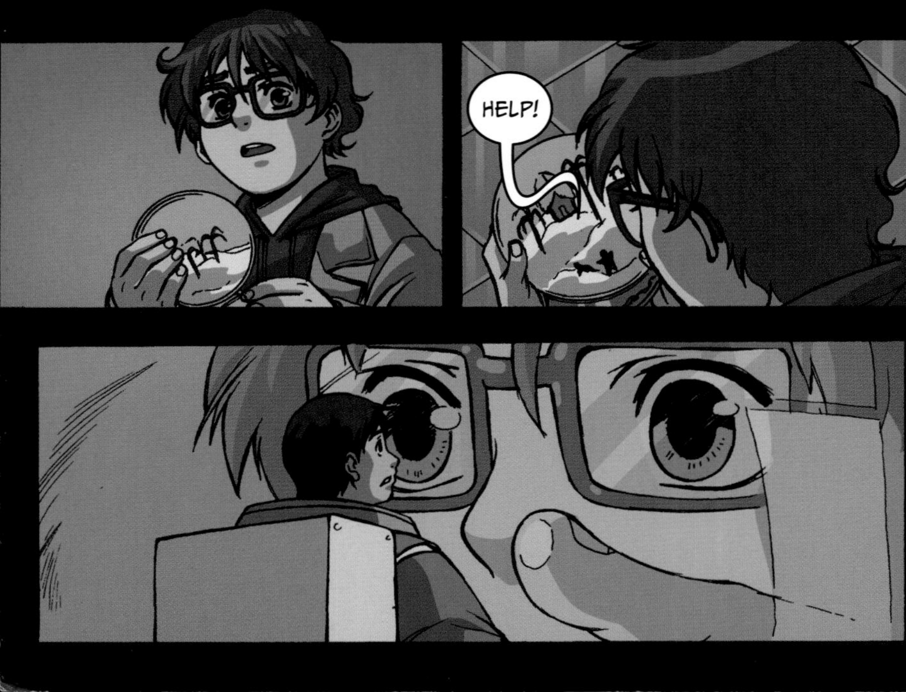
HELP!

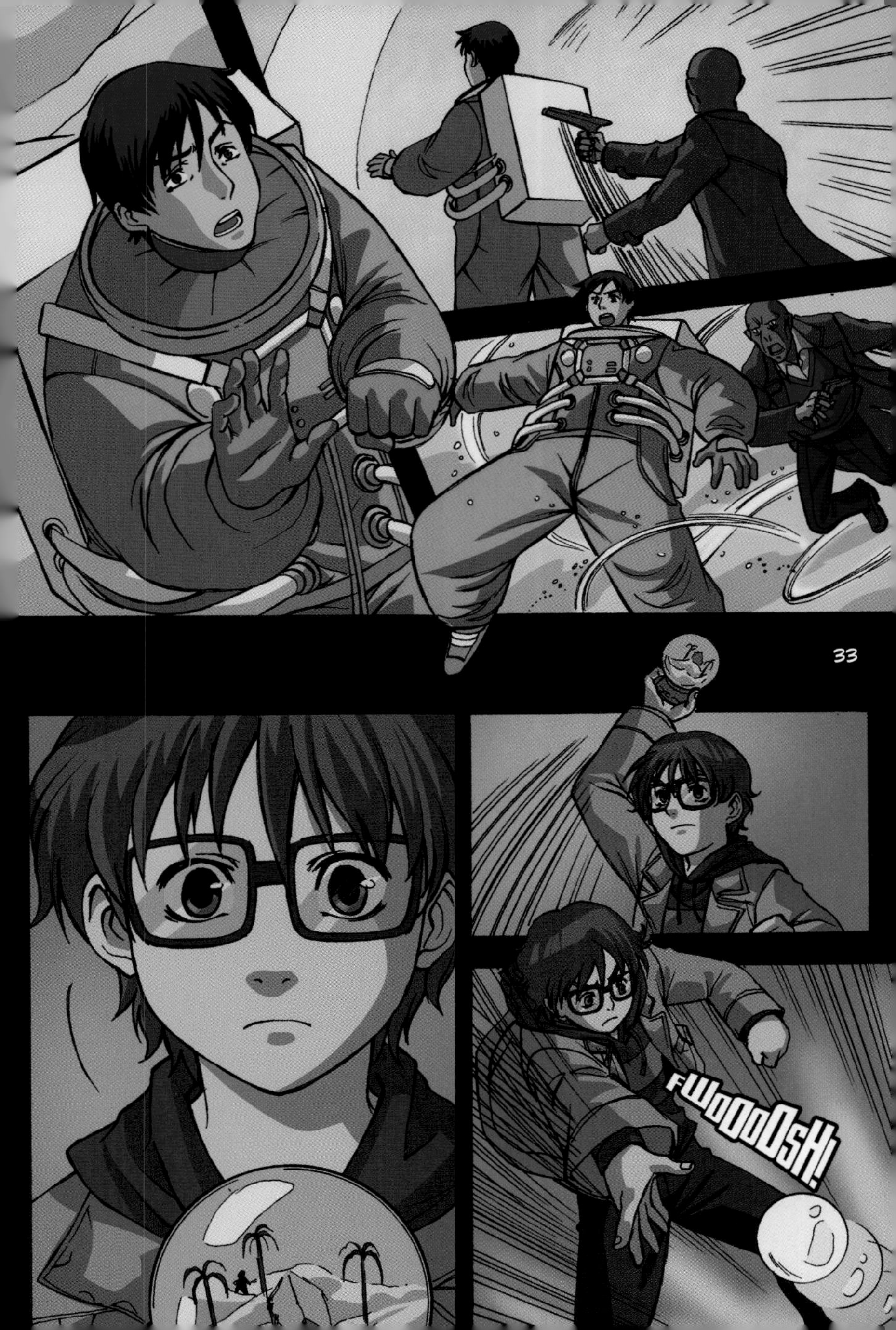
FWOOOOSH!

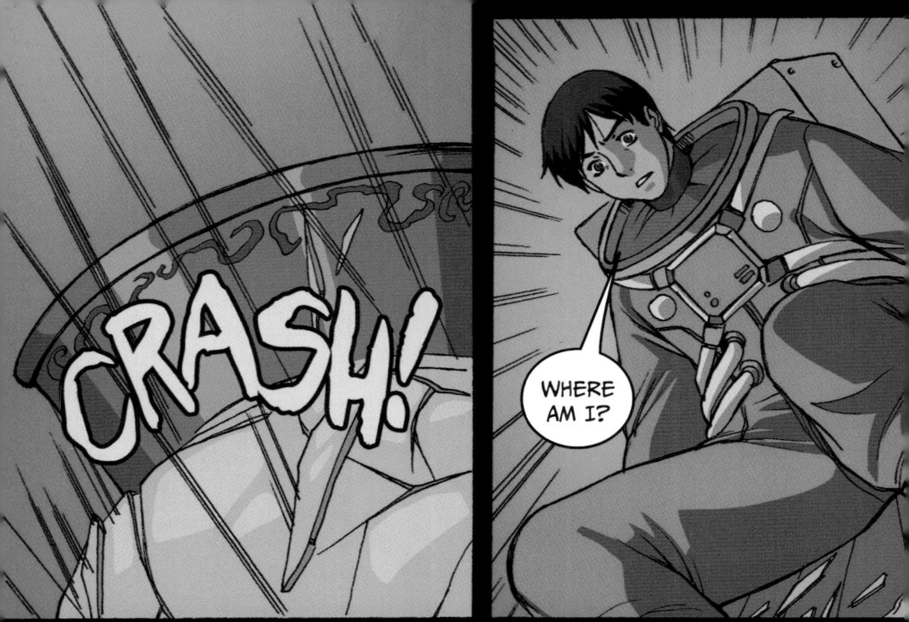
CRASH!
WHERE AM I?

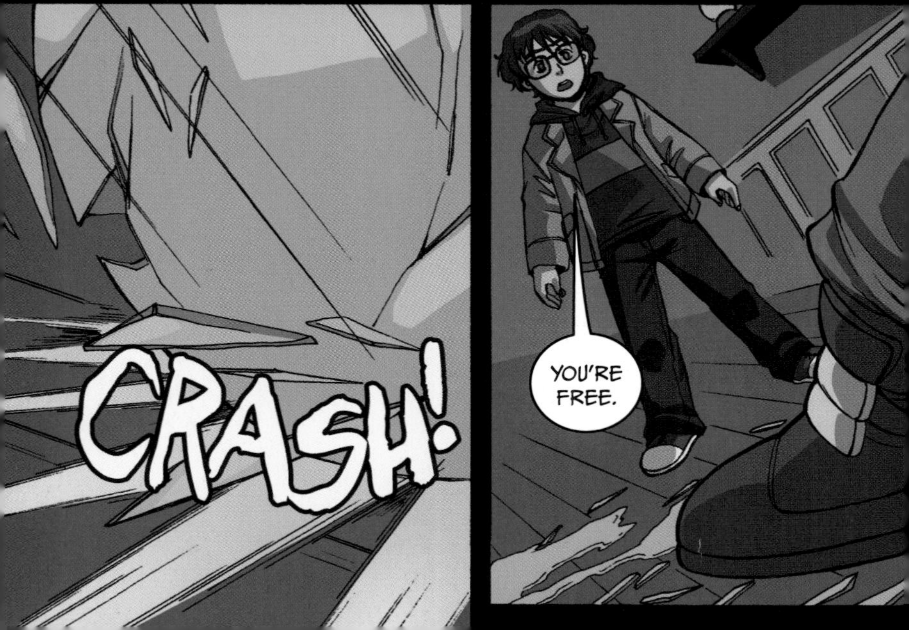
CRASH!
YOU'RE FREE.

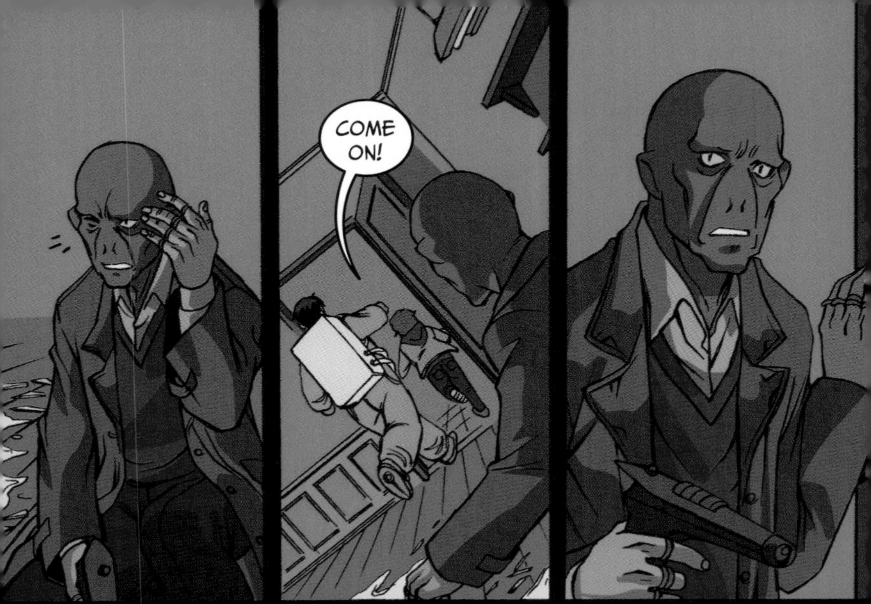
COME ON!

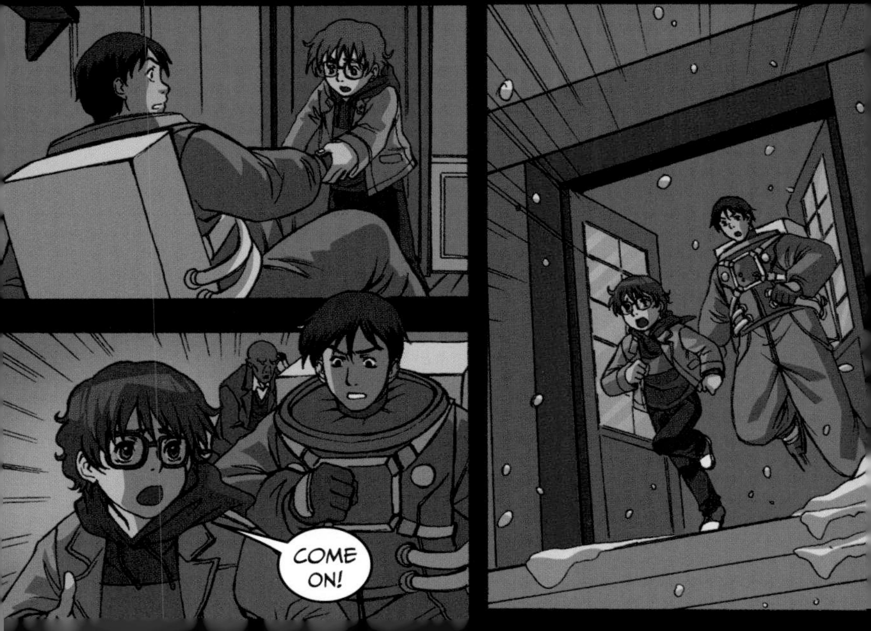
COME ON!

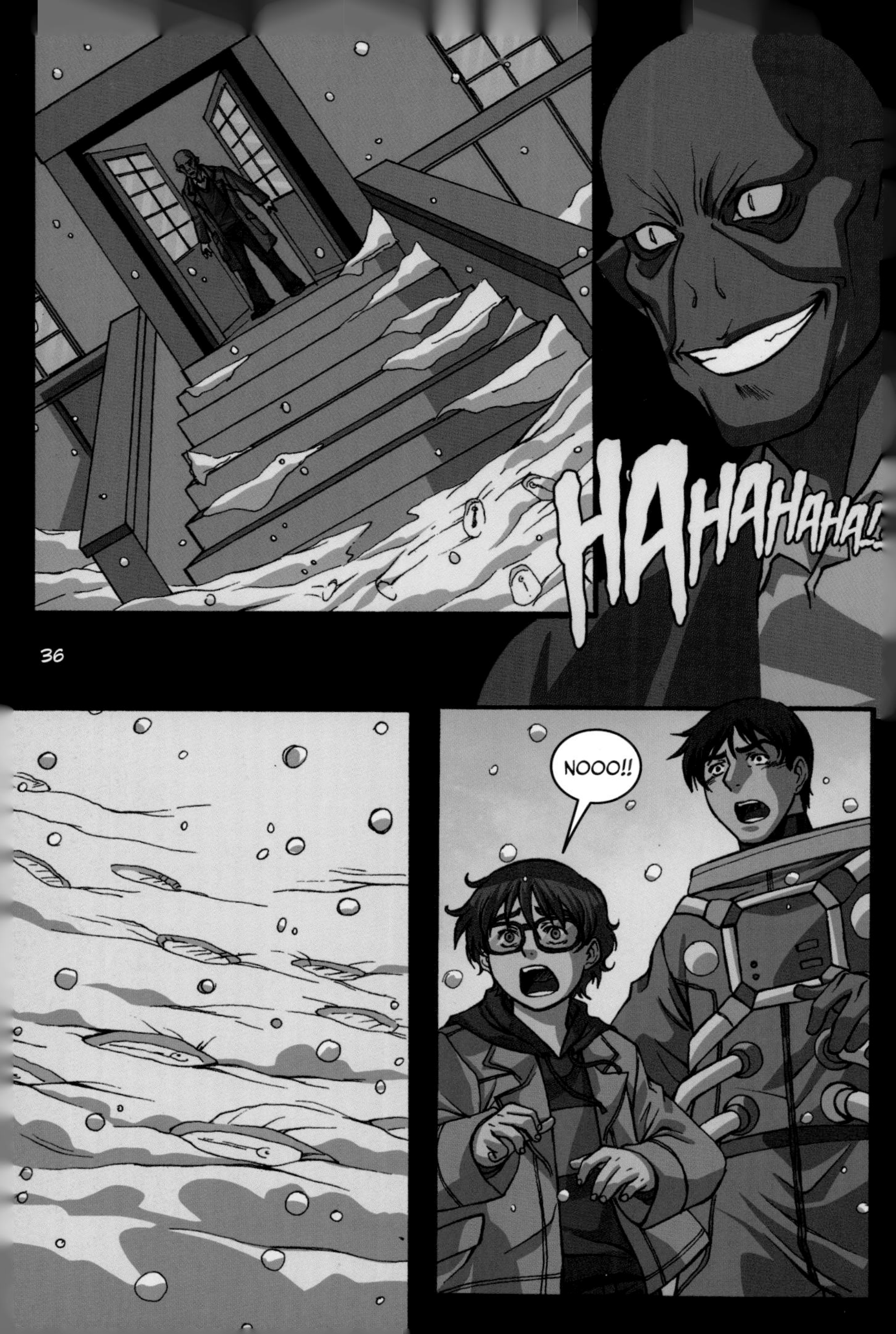
HAHAHAHAHA!!
NOOO!!

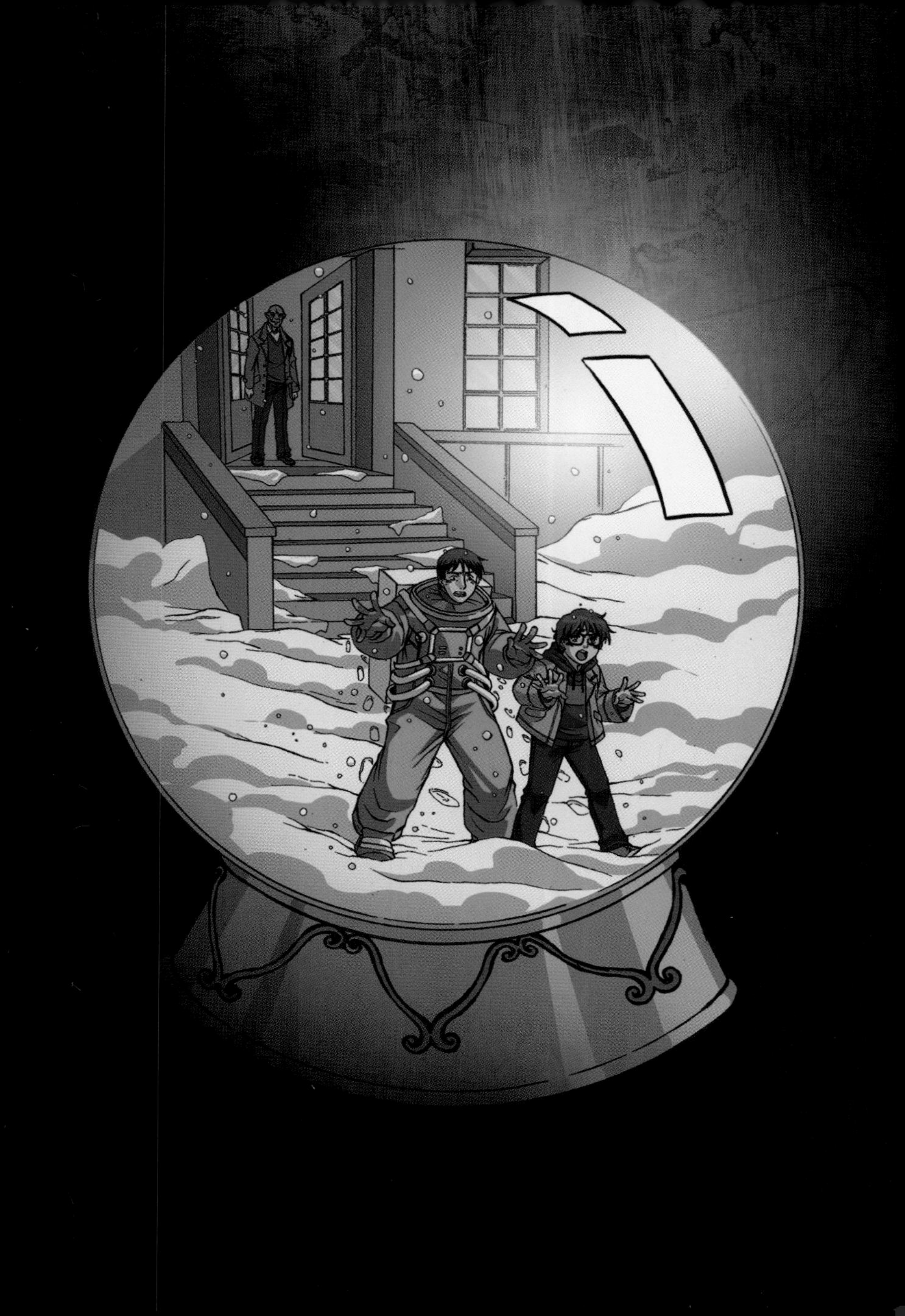

SCRIPT BY

Michael Dahl is the author of more than 200 books for
children and young adults. He has won the AEP Distinguished
Achievement Award three times for his non-fiction. His
Finnegan Zwake mystery series was shortlisted twice by
the Anthony and Agatha awards. He has also written the
Library of Doom series and the Dragonblood books. He is
a featured speaker at conferences around the country on
graphic novels and high-interest books for boys.

VISUAL GLOSSARY

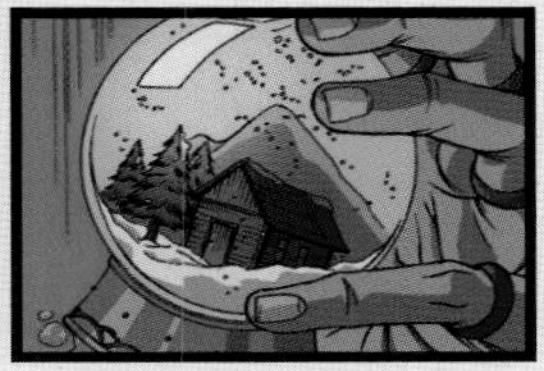

SNOW GLOBE

Authors of sci-fi and horror stories often begin their tales with a familiar setting or a harmless object, tricking the reader into thinking the story will be cozy and tame.

MOON LANDER

Authors and illustrators give clues about when a story takes place. The first moon lander flew into space in 1969. This story could not take place before that date.

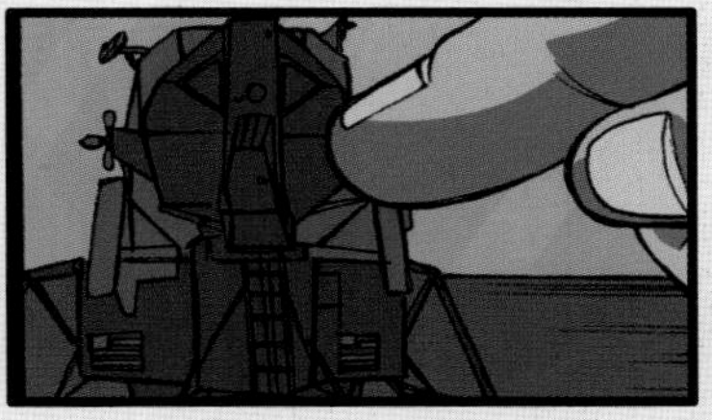

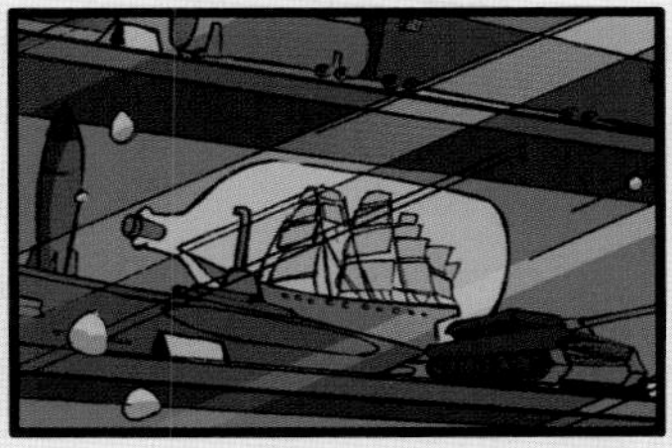

SHIP IN A BOTTLE

In the antique store, we see an old-fashioned ship in a bottle. This is an example of visual foreshadowing, a hint that something similar may happen later on: something, or someone, will end up imprisoned in glass.

LINES OF FORCE

In many graphic novels, "action lines" or "lines of force" are displayed around a character to highlight action or a dramatic moment and increase the tension.

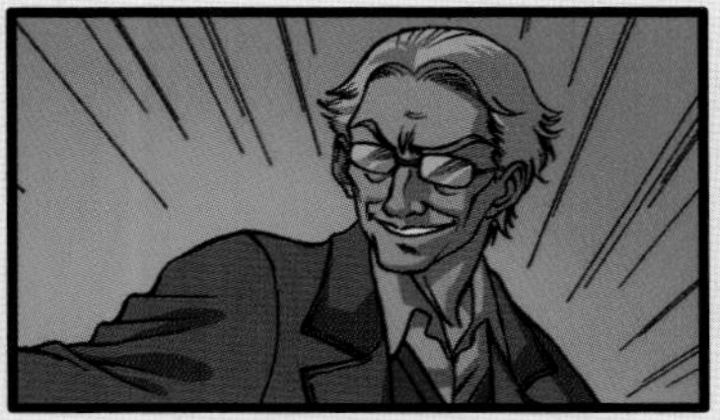

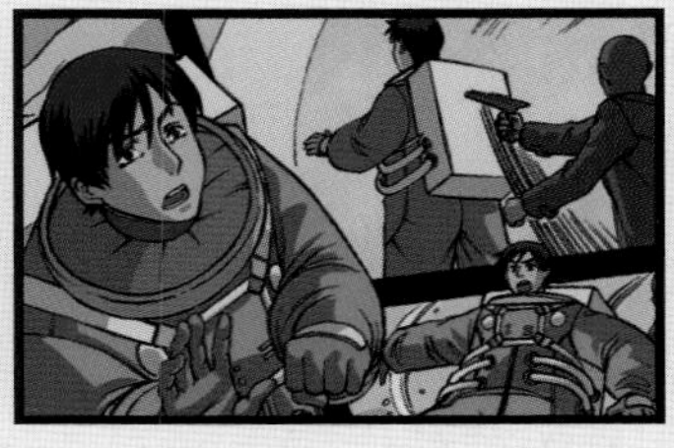

MULTIPLE FIGURES

In some graphic novel panels, we may see multiple versions of a single character. This gives the reader different perspectives or "camera angles" of a single action, and also implies rapid action.

VISUAL QUESTIONS

1. When the young boy notices the ax blade hissing in the snow, it gives him an idea about how to escape. But what makes the blade warm? Why was it not steaming when the boy picked it up earlier?

2. The alien shopkeeper has the power to shrink humans. Do you think he has other abilities? Look at other panels in the story for clues.

3. On page 20, although the shopkeeper appears to be standing still, we see that the boy is being hurled around inside the snow globe. Why?

4. A snowflake appears in the shopkeeper's eye. A snowflake lands on the boy's hand. Why do you think the illustrator shows these two things happening at the same time?

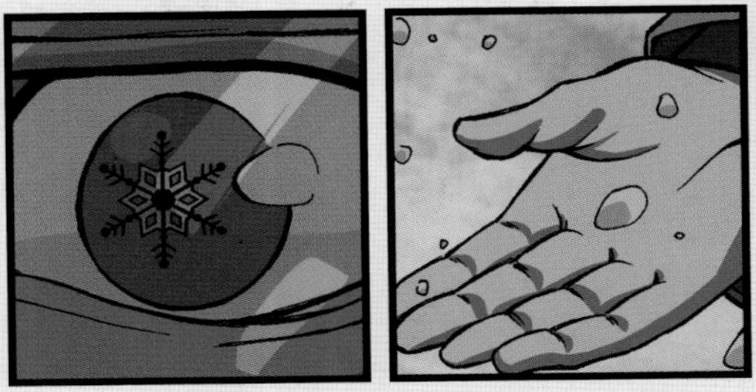

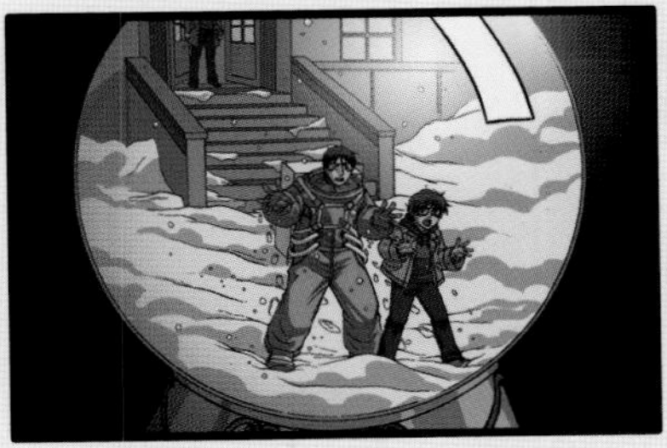

5. What happens at the end of the story? What is the illustrator telling us by making the final panel look like a snow globe?

6. Titles can tell us more than we realize. Look at the words ALIEN SNOW. If the two words were run together, might there be a second possible title? (Or say the title very slowly. You can hear a third, even creepier, title!)

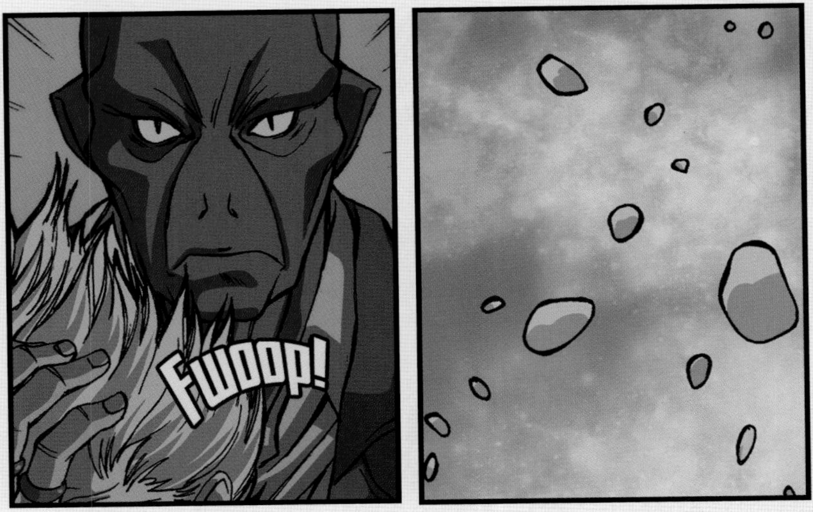
FWOOP!

CREATING THE BOOK

THE MANUSCRIPT

Graphic novels are often created by two different people –
a writer and an illustrator. Even when a book contains few
words, the writer must provide detailed notes called "scene
descriptions," instructing the content of each panel.

A page from the *Alien Snow* manuscript:

PAGE 18

Panel 1
Shopkeeper walks down busy street. Cars and trucks zip
by.

SFX: HONK! HONK!

Panel 2
People pass by, some are walking pets, some are talking
on cell phones.

Panel 3
Shopkeeper turns on to quieter city street.

Panel 4
The boy being whipped around inside of the snow-globe
prison.

Noah: WHOA!

Panel 5
Boy holds his hands to his ears. The globe is surrounded
by loud, amplified sounds coming from outside.

SFX: HONK! HONK!

Panel 6
Close-up of boy wondering where he is now.

PENCILS

After receiving the manuscript from the writer, the illustrator creates rough sketches called "pencils." The writer and editor of the book review these drawings, making sure all corrections are made before continuing to the next stage.

From page 18 of *Alien Snow*:

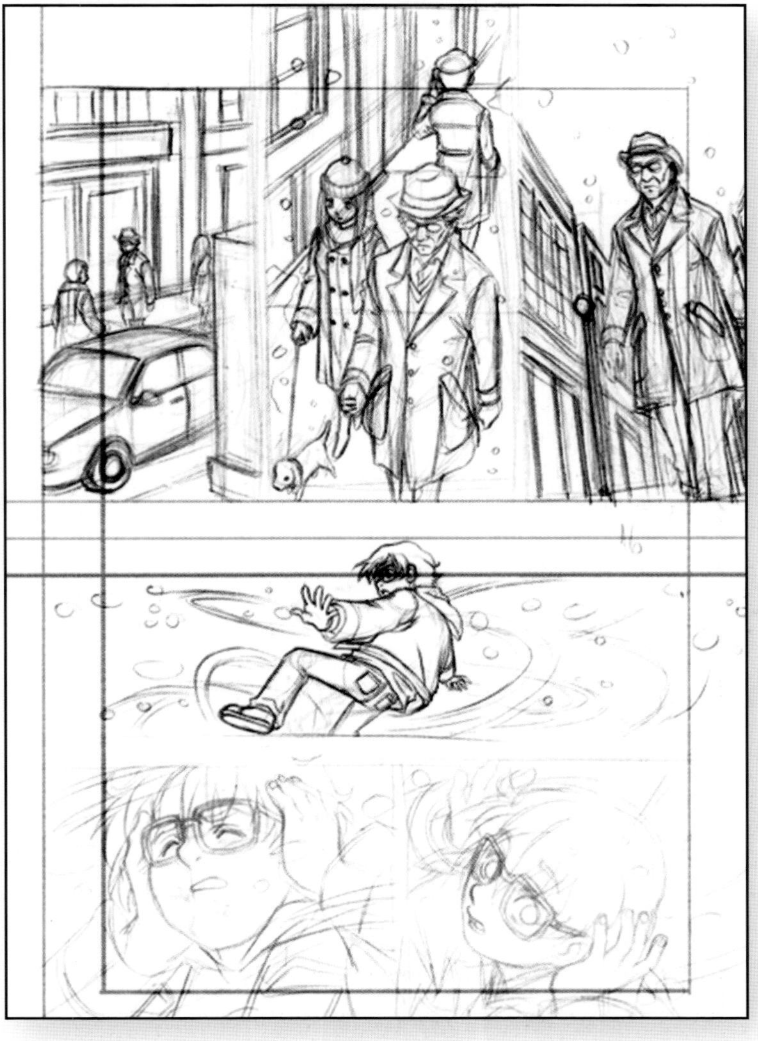

INKS

When illustrations have been approved by the editor, an artist, sometimes called an "inker," draws over the pencils in ink. This stage allows readers to see the illustration more easily in print.

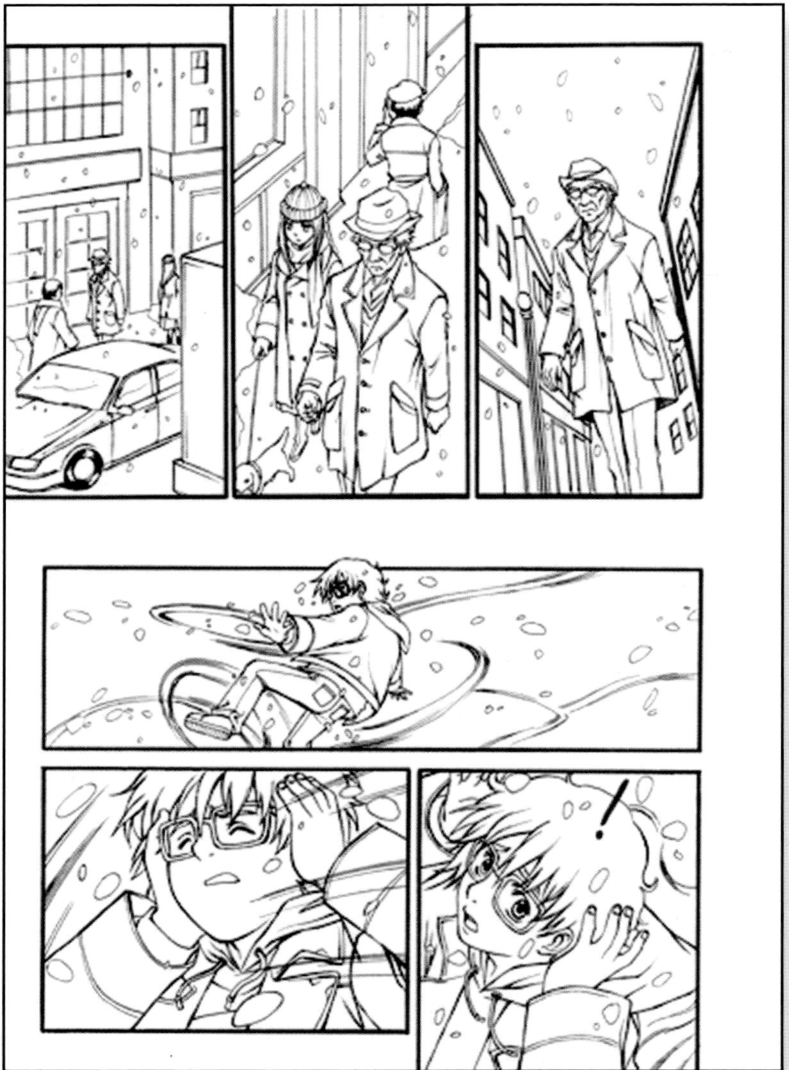

!

COLORS

Next, the inks are sent to a "colorist" who adds color to each panel of art.

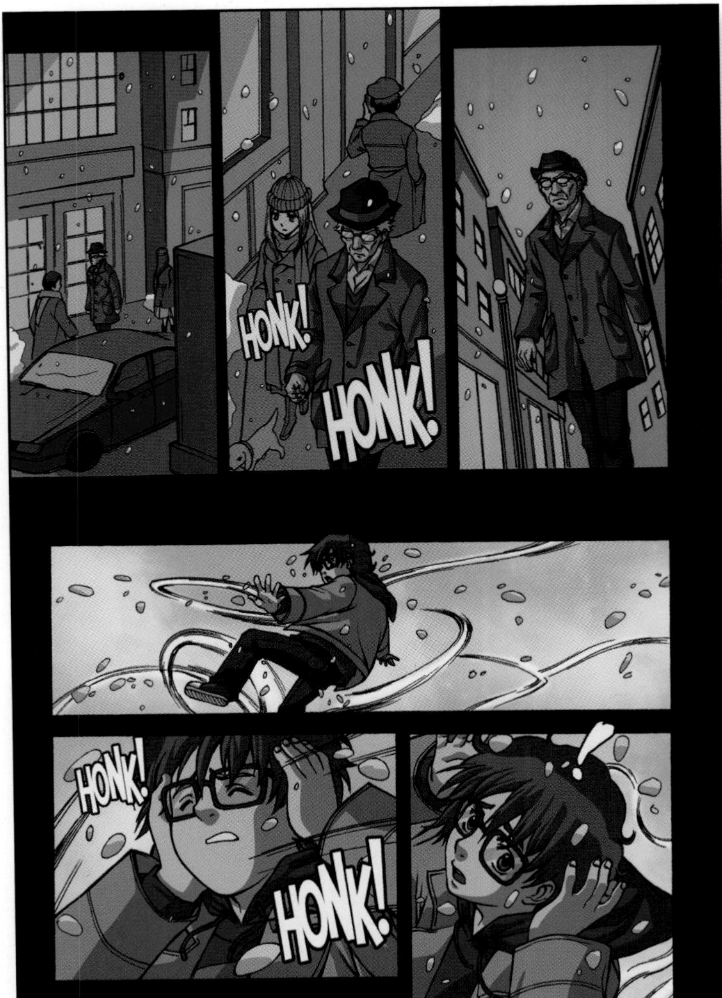
HONK!
HONK!
HONK!
HONK!

When the art is completed, designers add the final touches, including word balloons and sound effects. Turn to page 18 to see the final version.

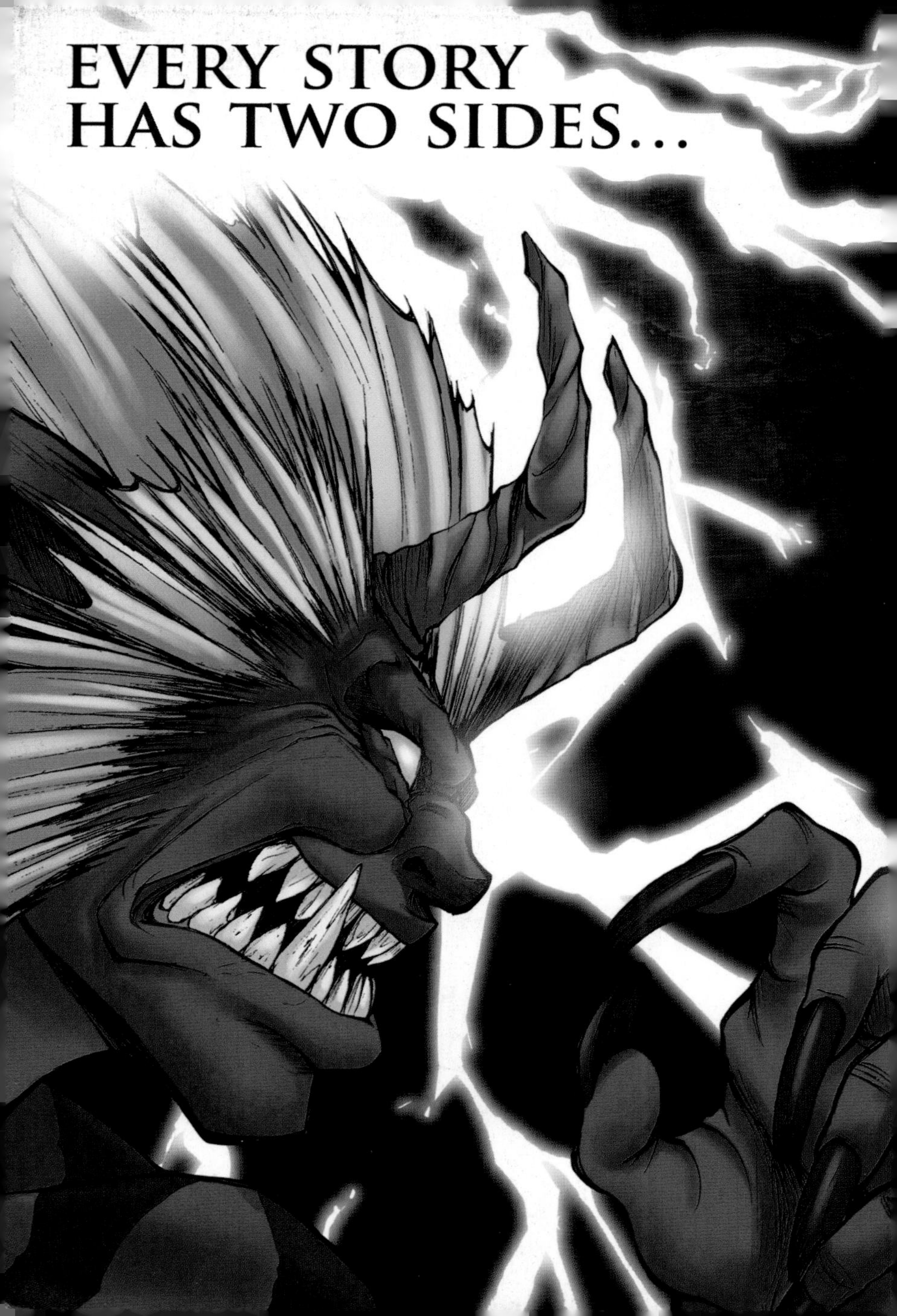
EVERY STORY
HAS TWO SIDES...

GOOD VS EVIL

Adventure

DIVER DOWN
Lemke · Yonami
GOOD VS EVIL

Fantasy

DUNGEON OF SEVEN DOOMS
Dahl · Pares
GOOD VS EVIL

Science Fiction

ALIEN SNOW
Dahl · Pares
GOOD VS EVIL

Horror

THE AWAKENING
Lemke · Medeiros
GOOD VS EVIL

COLLECT THEM ALL!

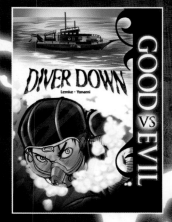

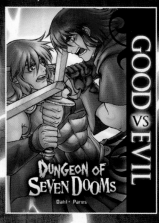

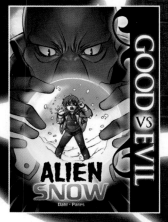

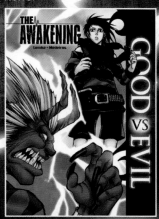

GOOD vs EVIL